posies and poison

Sweetfern Harbor Cozy Mystery - 1

wendy meadows

Majestic Owl Publishing LLC
P.O. Box 997
Newport, NH 03773

 Created with Vellum

chapter one

Brenda Sheffield had surprised even herself when she decided to move from her home state of Michigan to the eastern seaboard. Sweetfern Harbor was a coastal New England town that held pleasant memories of when, as a ten-year-old, she had visited with her parents. Her most vivid memory was of her uncle's massive seaside home. Randolph Sheffield had managed to survive three unsuccessful marriages, and with no offspring. He had shown Brenda special attention during their visit and she recalled her mother commenting more than once that she had never before known her brother-in-law to show any enthusiasm over a child.

"I think he liked how excited Brenda was about the enormous house," said Ellen. Her father had merely raised his eyebrows.

Brenda smiled to herself as her car took the next curve. Since her mother's death, she had not thought back to that magical excursion to Sweetfern Harbor until the letter from the lawyer arrived. It was delivered with instructions to sign to confirm that she received it.

When she was in her teens she learned that her uncle had decided to turn his mansion into a bed and breakfast. At the time, Brenda found the idea somewhat intriguing, but quickly grew disinterested when her parents only wanted to discuss mundane details of business ventures instead of lingering on Brenda's preferred topic, the beauty and grandeur of Uncle Randolph's house itself.

After the next bend in the road, Brenda gasped at the beauty of the panorama before her. She pulled over to park at the overlook where she could get a better view. Rolling hills unfolded before her eyes until they reached a jagged coastline below. She had to tear herself away from the sight and got back into the car reluctantly. She was only one mile from her final destination and tingling with anticipation. As she started the car again, she gulped several times. Moisture slicked her hands on the steering wheel. At age forty-six, Brenda Sheffield was about to become the owner of Sweetfern Harbor's only bed and breakfast.

When Brenda decided to move to Sweetfern Harbor, she had left a modest job as assistant to the private investigator of a detective agency back in Michigan. She often studied cases on her own when she was home.

Rarely did her boss ask for her advice, but when he did, Brenda had several times provided an insight which propelled him toward a successful ending to the case. The humdrum daily tasks assigned to her were a sad waste of her talents.

She knew she was good in this line of work, but her boss had never acknowledged her contributions other than a muttered "Thanks" when she provided input. Young and upcoming Jason Kirkpatrick displayed an arrogance that made Brenda feel more than a little inferior, and eager for change.

The letter from her uncle's lawyer came at the right time for her. Even though she had no idea how to run a bed and breakfast, the thought of living in that stately mansion so close to the ocean drove her to a confidence that propelled her from Michigan all the way to the Atlantic Ocean.

But her confidence sometimes wavered, even to this moment. It was too late for doubts, she reminded herself. All she could do at this point was hope she had a good staff already in place, and forge ahead.

Entering town, Brenda coasted down the slight incline onto a street out of a fairy tale. In the bright sunshine, hanging baskets of brilliant flowers hung outside every shop. The many hues of the cascading flowers flanked doorways with shingle signs rocking softly in the Atlantic breeze.

The panorama before her gave her a thrill of pleasure, but for some reason it also increased her anxiety. She wondered if she would fit in to such a place. Misgivings surged through her as she remembered how her boss back in Michigan laughed when she told him of her plans.

She eagerly read the name of each establishment she passed. Morning Sun Coffee caught her eye. She wanted nothing more than to go inside, sit down, and sip a cup of hot coffee. She would ask for her favorite flavor shot, caramel, and its delicious richness might just be enough to chase away the knot of worry in her stomach.

Brushing aside this desire, she lowered her window and breathed in the gentle sea air and listened to faint sounds of surging water. At the end of Main Street, she turned right and followed Ocean Street until one block later she came to her destination.

The huge mansion was pale yellow, four stories tall, and as magnificent as she recalled from her childhood. She slowed down to take in the stately Victorian house, which the lawyer had informed her was a Queen Anne from the 1890s or so. She vowed to examine her deed in greater detail as soon as possible to be sure of its age.

A sign swung from wrought iron hooks on the beam of the

porch, welcoming everyone to Sheffield Bed and Breakfast. Her eyes shifted upward to the fourth floor. Memories flooded over her. She recalled that was where her Uncle Randolph had opened cabinets built into the walls and showed her a dollhouse and its antique figurines. She had spent hours playing there until her mother insisted she come downstairs and mind her manners in front of her uncle. Randolph's kind eyes told Brenda that her uncle gained more pleasure in her delight than in her efforts to listen to adults' boring conversations.

Brenda knew from the initial letter from her uncle's estate lawyer, Edward Graham, that the grand house consisted of eight bedrooms and two apartments. One would be hers and the other one was occupied by the live-in housekeeper. There seemed to be no problem keeping the rooms occupied most seasons of the year, according to the lawyer.

As she gazed at the house's intricate details, she could see a line of tall pine trees that wrapped halfway around the structure. As tall as they were, the trees failed to overpower the building in the slightest. The house, with its gracefully detailed trim, wide wraparound porches, and gabled roof with a quaint tower in one corner, rose prominently over the street.

She stepped from her car and the sound of the ocean grew louder. She walked across the vast lawn of the property and shielded her eyes against the bright sun to view the water crashing against the rocks below. Screaming seagulls coasted on the wind, vying for their meal. The view took her breath away. The bright expanse of the ocean extended as far as her eyes could see.

"You must be Miss Sheffield," she heard behind her, and turned around quickly. "I'm Phyllis Lindsey, your housekeeper." The fifty-something-year-old woman extended her hand. A smile spread on her thin lips and her deep gray eyes were friendly.

"Yes, I'm Brenda Sheffield. I'm happy to meet you." Right

away, Brenda felt a kinship with the housekeeper. Phyllis was trim and wore a simple skirt below her knees and a sensible white blouse, perfectly pressed.

Together, they turned to walk toward the bed and breakfast. "Everyone is very anxious to meet you. Mr. Sheffield hired all of the employees personally." She clucked her tongue. "We were so sorry to lose him. His sudden illness hit him hard and he just never recovered." She glanced quickly at Brenda. "Oh, I'm so sorry. I only meant to convey how much he meant to all of us. I am very sorry for your loss."

Brenda smiled at her. "It's all right. I only met him once when I was ten years old, but my parents kept in contact with him over the years."

She took a long breath and looked again at her new home. Brenda pushed away feelings of unease about her new responsibilities. This venture was not leading her to a career as a sleuth, which had been her longtime dream. But surely living in Sweetfern Harbor would give her time to really figure out her life.

As Phyllis led Brenda up the graceful stairs to the main entrance, a young woman stepped forward. The light that filtered through the oval glass door pane highlighted her light auburn hair and crystal blue eyes. Phyllis stepped forward to make the introductions.

"This is Carrie Martin. Carrie is eighteen and a quick learner," said Phyllis. "She manages the office and takes care of the room reservations."

Another young woman emerged from behind Carrie with a wave. "And this is my cousin Kelly Martin. Kelly is visiting me from New York City," said Carrie. "If you prefer to get settled into your quarters first, I'll see to some refreshments," offered Phyllis.

It was decided that Carrie would show Brenda up to her apartment. When they arrived at the second floor, Brenda followed her to the end of the hallway. There Carrie opened a door with a key and then handed it to Brenda.

From the entrance, a few steps brought her down to a cozy sitting area. Beyond this, Brenda could see a comfortably appointed bedroom and adjoining bath. There was an alcove off the sitting room with a coffeepot, toaster, and microwave. Her new living space reminded her exactly of her childhood visit, with its beautiful antique furniture that gleamed with polish in the light filtering through a lace curtain at the window.

"Mr. Sheffield did not want a stove or oven in here. He preferred to eat all meals with his staff or his guests." Carrie glanced at Brenda. "Of course, that will be your own choice now."

"This is just lovely. I'll freshen up and meet you downstairs soon." Brenda smiled at Carrie. She was pleased with the young girl's hospitality skills and immediately understood why guests felt so at home here.

Once the four women were settled in the formal but cozy sitting room on the first floor, Brenda could sense their curiosity about her circumstances. She helped herself to a shortbread cookie from the delicate china plate that Phyllis had placed on a doily in the center of the mahogany table.

"I suppose it was difficult leaving your family behind in Michigan," said Phyllis, handing her a glass of iced tea.

"I have no family left there," Brenda explained, gratefully accepting the glass and taking a sip. "My mother passed away in a car accident ten years ago."

There was a slight pause as the other women gave her looks of sympathy, but somehow Brenda knew none of them would hold back their curiosity.

"What kind of work did you do back in Michigan?" asked Carrie, passing a cookie to her cousin Kelly.

"I worked for a private investigator as his assistant. On occasion, I helped with some of his cases." There was no reason for her to embellish or diminish the explanation. "I guess you could say I am something of an amateur sleuth."

Phyllis laughed good-naturedly. "Well, those skills won't be needed in Sweetfern Harbor. I don't recall any crimes around here in the time I've been here." Carrie readily agreed. Phyllis continued, "We are known to be the safest town in all of New England."

The longer they chatted, the more relaxed Brenda became. She was happy there was no crime here. She thought that if crime prevailed, it would spoil her initial impressions of the village. Turning her mind from thoughts of her detective ambitions, she turned to ask Phyllis another question. "I noticed the coffee shop in town. All of the shops looked so inviting and quaint."

She was told about the florist, the bakery, and other specialty shops. As the other visitor, Kelly sat back and listened along with Brenda to this happy chatter. Phyllis and Carrie tended to interrupt one another telling her who owned which shop and how the relationships between the townspeople intertwined with one another. Regardless of blood relations, apparently Sweetfern Harbor was one big happy family.

"Are the owners lifelong residents here?" asked Brenda.

Phyllis and Carrie exchanged glances. Then Phyllis spoke. "No one owns the buildings, but they do own their businesses." At Brenda's quizzical look, Phyllis explained, "Your uncle owned this house and the land around it, of course. The Pendleton family owns just about everything else in town—but there's just the old woman left now, Lady Pendleton we call her." She paused for a moment. "If we didn't have the tourist industry, no one would be in business today with the rents so high." She stopped abruptly as if searching for a change of topic.

By her manner, Brenda could see the housekeeper did not wish to discuss Lady Pendleton any further. Without a doubt, this formidable woman was not to be considered a part of the Sweetfern Harbor family.

"We get a lot of tourists down here," Carrie jumped in, eager to steer the conversation back to safer ground. "They love how colorful Main Street is…and the ocean, of course." Carrie told stories about the beach parties she and her friends enjoyed during her recent high school years. "You won't have to leave Sweetfern Harbor for a vacation. The sandy beach is a wonderful place for relaxation." Phyllis nodded her head vigorously in agreement.

Brenda took a last sip of her iced tea and looked around at the women. "I should get unpacked and settled in." She turned to Carrie. "Perhaps tomorrow we can get together and I'll look over the books. I need to get a handle on the business part of the bed and breakfast first."

They all stood up. "Brenda, do you want to have your dinner brought up to your room later this evening?"

"I think I'd prefer to join the others. How many guests are here now?"

"Our rooms are filled for the next few weeks," said Carrie. "Dinner is served at seven. We'll see you then."

When she reached the top of the stairs, Brenda could hear soft voices below. She knew she was being assessed and hoped she passed whatever standard was expected of her. Then she smiled. Phyllis and Carrie had been so warm and friendly, she had no doubt she would fit in at Sheffield Bed and Breakfast.

But a little anxiety remained when she wondered about everyone else in Sweetfern Harbor. She also had an insatiable curiosity about Lady Pendleton. Before Phyllis stopped speaking on the subject, Brenda felt sure there was something more to Lady Pendleton's story.

Brenda laughed softly as she unlocked her new apartment and stepped inside. "I really must be careful of this kind of gossip or I will get a reputation before I've had a chance to prove myself around here."

After a sound sleep in her soft four-poster bed, Brenda came downstairs the next morning to the sounds of a male voice. Someone was teasing Carrie in the front reception area. The young woman's laugh echoed melodiously and Brenda was curious to find out who had brought out such merriment in her office manager.

"Good morning, Miss Sheffield," said Carrie, still smiling as Brenda joined them. "This is Logan Tucker. He works in the coffee shop you saw on your way into town yesterday." Logan's wide grin told Brenda he must be good with customers.

"It is very nice to meet you, Logan. I must stop in for one of your specialties soon. And, please, everyone, just call me Brenda. Miss Sheffield is too formal for me." She smiled in mock admonishment at Carrie, whose cheeks blushed a light pink.

Logan shook Brenda's hand. "I really admired your uncle, Miss—uh, Brenda. Mr. Sheffield and I became very close. He was my mentor."

"Good thing you had him to steer you back onto the right track," Carrie teased him, and Logan ducked his head with a grin.

"I'm glad to hear he was your mentor," Brenda said. "I only met him once, but I have such wonderful memories of him. I'm glad he was able to help you." Brenda looked expectantly at Carrie. "I'm going to have a little breakfast and then we can meet around nine, Carrie?"

"Sure," said Carrie. "I'll see you then." She and Logan turned back to their talk and teasing as Brenda headed for the dining room.

chapter two

By day three in Sweetfern Harbor, Brenda had learned the bed and breakfast operation from top to bottom. With such a capable staff, she realized she had no need to micromanage the everyday details, and so instead, she planned to spend the day exploring Main Street.

Thinking back to her first day, and how easily Phyllis had chatted to her about everyone in town, Brenda went to find the housekeeper after breakfast and told Phyllis her plans.

"I don't want to intrude, but if you'd like some company, I'll come along with you," Phyllis offered. "No need to be nervous, I can introduce you to everyone. My daughter, Molly, owns Morning Sun Coffee." Brenda smiled in relief at the thought of having a companion. "If you don't need Carrie, she can usually find time for a break and introduce you to her friends in town as well."

Since most of Carrie's work for the morning was already done, the excursion was quickly arranged. The three left the bed and breakfast and walked the block and a half to Main Street. Before they reached the coffee shop, several shop owners came out to greet Phyllis and eagerly introduced themselves to their new neighbor. The smalltown friendliness was almost overwhelming at first, but by the time they reached Morning Sun, Brenda had met so many smiling faces and accepted so many genuine offers to "Stop in some time, any time!" that she began to feel more at ease.

Molly's eyes lit up when they entered the Morning Sun, the bell at the shop door making its friendly jingle. Phyllis introduced her daughter to the new owner of Sheffield Bed and Breakfast. As Molly shook her hand, Brenda gazed around the warm interior, where people sat happily ensconced at little tables or booths with their drinks. Toward the back were several cozy armchairs where a few solo patrons sat to read their newspapers. Upbeat music played softly over the radio and it smelled invitingly of freshly roasted coffee beans.

"I've already heard a lot about you," said Molly. "Logan couldn't stop talking about you. That is, when he finally decided to come in for work." She laughed fondly. Logan, making a latté behind the counter, kept his eyes down at Molly's comment and did not look up. "Where do you want to sit?" asked Molly.

"By the window, of course," said Phyllis. "We don't want to miss anything going on outside."

Molly brought over a plain black coffee for her mother and a latté for Carrie, and set a fragrant, steaming mug in front of Brenda. "Vanilla latté, our specialty, as requested," she said. "I hope you like it. I'll send Logan over with a bite to eat in just a moment."

Molly hurried off to help her other customers and the three women sat sipping their drinks and watching as tourists strolled by on the sidewalk outside. A couple sat down at the table next to theirs.

"I don't know how I'm going to survive another raise in rent. That woman has enough money without squeezing more from everyone in town." Brenda's eyes widened. They tried not to listen, but the couple's talk was drowned out a moment later by the jangling door bell. A large group of tourists had all trooped into the coffee shop at once.

Phyllis shook her head and frowned, leaning forward. "They must mean Lady Pendleton. Molly said something about it to me yesterday. Lady Pendleton came around to tell everyone to expect another increase. She just increased them two months ago! There ought to be a law against that."

"She will keep doing it until there's no businesses left in town," said Carrie. "I wonder if she's thought about that. No businesses would mean no rent and the whole town would die." Brenda was puzzled by Carrie's tone, which seemed far too bitter for one so young.

Logan approached their table with a plate of delectable poppy seed scones. "Maybe she doesn't care if everyone goes out of business," he commented, apparently all too familiar with this topic. "Maybe she wants to be all alone on her heap of money up in that mansion." He set down the plate and winked at Carrie before heading back to the coffee bar.

Phyllis shook her head. "That's not it. The property is what seems to give her lordship over everyone: not the money, but knowing she owns it all."

Molly, having returned to top off her mother's coffee, also overheard their conversation. "She gets a real kick out of causing hardship for others. She has no heart whatsoever."

"Alright already," exclaimed Brenda. "Who is this ogre who seems to rule everyone around here?" This was all the prodding they needed to expound on Lady Pendleton.

"I don't think anyone knows her first name," Molly said.

"I think she likes that her name has been forgotten over the years," said Carrie with a melancholy sigh. "It is kind of old-fashioned and romantic, even for a real estate ogre, don't you think?" Carrie rolled her eyes.

"Well, she prefers to be called Lady Pendleton, I know that much. She gave me a talking-to one time when I called her Mrs.

Pendleton. I'll never forget that," said Molly. "Here's the funny thing, though. She's married to a man the complete opposite of her. From what I've heard, he has a modest pension. He manages to live mentally and emotionally apart from his wife. William is his name. He married into her family's money and has no control over what his wife does in her business dealings."

"He is a shy man but very nice to everyone he meets. I don't understand why he's still with her," said Carrie. "He could do so much better for himself."

The others nodded. Phyllis stirred her fresh cup of black coffee. Brenda noted Phyllis's face had remained blank the whole time—except when Molly had spoken William Pendleton's name. A soft fold had appeared at the corners of her mouth, like the suggestion of a smile.

Everyone glanced toward the door as the bell jingled again. Molly's face lit up. Phyllis leaned closer to Brenda. "That's Molly's boyfriend, Pete Graham. He's the mailman, too."

Pete hurried over to greet Molly and handed her a short stack of mail. "I brought this by from your post office box to save you time going to fetch it."

Molly's gaze was glued to Pete's for an instant. She thanked him and introduced him to Brenda. As they shook hands she saw his eyes were almost navy blue. A hank of dark hair nearly covered his right eye and he brushed it back. He was tall compared to Molly's petite, tanned frame.

As it turned out, Pete brought more than just the mail. "I guess you heard what her ladyship is doing now," he said. They nodded. "I heard she is ready to evict the Swansons out on Hideaway Road. They were a hundred dollars short on rent and she refused to wait until the end of the week for the balance. She's already sent the authorities out there to serve eviction papers. They have two days to get out."

Looks of sadness and consternation flooded the faces of everyone around Brenda. Then Carrie spoke up.

"Why doesn't your father do something about that woman? He's her lawyer. How can he stand by and watch this? Surely he can get her to stop this madness. The Swansons have four small children. Where will they go?"

It dawned on Brenda that Pete Graham was the son of the lawyer she dealt with in the matter of inheriting her uncle's estate and the Sheffield Bed and Breakfast. Knowing the care and concern he had demonstrated with her simple questions, she thought Carrie made a good point.

"The only reason my father keeps her as a client is so that she won't go to some high-powered lawyers who will go along with everything she wants. At least my father stands up to her sometimes. But he's not a miracle worker." Pete knew the rationalization was lame but it was all he could offer. "It's not only the Swansons who will be affected, she is coming down hard on two more families out on Hideaway Road. I don't know where it will all end but I'll keep you posted on that."

Brenda made a mental note to not give out confidential information about the bed and breakfast. Small-town friendliness came at a cost, she realized. If the day came when Pete Graham had anything against her, she knew how damaging it would be.

She decided she would need to emphasize to Carrie later, in private, to not divulge the business's financial information to anyone around town. She wondered how that would fly.

When the three women left Morning Sun, they stopped at Sweet Treats Bakery a few doors down. "This is where we get our pastries and baked goods for the bed and breakfast," explained Carrie, opening the glass front door of the shop. "Hope bakes everything on the premises daily." Brenda's mouth watered thinking of the fresh sesame seed bagel she enjoyed earlier at breakfast.

Hope greeted them with a broad smile and insisted they sample the petit fours she had just finished decorating with dainty icing flowers. No one could resist, and the confections were richly flavored but light on the tongue. "These are incredible," Brenda marveled.

"Exactly. The guests rave about our breakfasts and desserts. Hope is our secret weapon," Carrie said with a grin.

Their next stop was Jenny's Blossoms, a shop at the quieter end of the main road. The display windows held meticulously arranged bouquets of daisies and a deep pink flower Brenda couldn't name but instantly coveted for her bedside table. Jenny Rivers, the owner, greeted them with enthusiasm. "No introduction necessary, Phyllis. Hello, Brenda. I'm so happy to meet Randolph Sheffield's niece at last." Brenda smiled back at her friendly greeting as they shook hands.

"I will be happy to keep providing flowers for Sheffield Bed and Breakfast. I presume you will also continue weddings and other events there as well?" Brenda nodded and reassured her things would proceed as they always had, having been briefed by Carrie on her second day about how such special events could be counted on to provide extra income. Jenny smiled to hear this news, then changed the subject and directed her next remarks to Phyllis and Carrie.

"I suppose you heard about the Swansons. As usual, Lady Pendleton seems bent on making everyone's lives miserable." They all nodded. "I hear she is greedier than ever," Jenny confided. "I don't know how she expects people to keep up. She just raised rents on all the shops on Main Street. I wish just a drop of human kindness would enter into her heart..." As she said this, she looked down, evidently no longer trading in light gossip.

Brenda was not surprised to discover that the blonde, energetic owner of Jenny's Blossoms knew as much gossip as Pete Graham. But she was surprised to learn that under the surface of this everyday gossip lurked a much darker, sadder reality for the shopkeeper.

"It's not just the rents, though. Did you hear she won that big court battle last week and has already introduced another one?" Tears sprang to Jenny's eyes. "Now she has filed a suit against me. She claims the backed-up plumbing in here is my fault and she's suing me for the cost to fix it." Phyllis reached for Jenny's hand and Carrie made a sound of distress as she put her arm around their friend's shoulders to comfort her.

Jenny looked up at Brenda. "Oh dear, I didn't want to ruin your welcome, Brenda, but this is just too much. This is my busy season. We have events and parties and tourists all over the place but I have fixed expenses, and you can't squeeze blood from a stone. I simply can't keep up with the higher rent and also pay for this plumbing fiasco. I don't know what I'm going to do."

"Carrie here was just asking Pete this morning why he can't ask his father to do something about her. Edward Graham should take responsibility for Lady Pendleton if she's going to prey on the whole town," said Phyllis. Carrie nodded as she hugged Jenny. "Something ought to be done to stop her and that's all there is to it."

Brenda watched Phyllis set her mouth in a firm line as she said this, but the older woman's eyes drifted to the window as if she lacked the conviction of her strong words.

"I may be new to town, but in just a few short days it seems like she's all I've heard about. It's sad this beautiful place has such a dark shadow hanging over it," said Brenda.

With a few last hugs and reassurances, they said their goodbyes to Jenny and reassured her the whole town was on her side. "The town needs to get together and figure something out," said Phyllis.

When they exited the shop into the bright sunshine, Brenda felt the tingle of exhaustion in her brain. She realized Sweetfern Harbor did not need a newspaper. In fact, when it came to local news, no one needed the internet, or the local news channels either.

"Jenny may be a little excitable, but this is beyond all reason. I don't know how Lady Pendleton could think a sweet girl like her is at fault for the rotten old plumbing in that building," said Phyllis as they walked back along Main Street. "You know, Jenny spent a lot of time at our house in the past. She and my Molly are best friends, along with Hope from the bakery. Of course, that was in my old house. I lost my home and my little business that I used to run, thanks to Lady Pendleton. Thankfully, your uncle hired me when he found out what happened. He had that empty attached apartment behind the main part of the bed and breakfast so he let me live there. It comes with the job. I don't know what I would have done without Randolph."

Phyllis sighed, and Brenda caught a glimpse of Carrie's sorrowful face as she listened to this—no doubt—familiar story. "I loved my shop. Molly tested out her first business idea when she opened a corner of it for coffee. I filled the place with beads and bobbles, as they say. I held classes for anyone who wanted to come in and make their own jewelry. Until she raised the rent just high enough that I couldn't afford it. She sent me a letter offering to buy my house, saying I could rent the crummy little apartment above the shop instead. I thought with the money from the sale of the house I could make it work, but then wouldn't you know those rents just crept up and up and up until I lost everything. That's when your uncle stepped in." Her shoulders sagged. "I can't keep crying over spilled milk, can I?" She turned to reassure Brenda. "But you must know I love working at Sheffield Bed and Breakfast so don't think I'll be leaving you any time soon."

Brenda squeezed Phyllis's hand in thanks. The more she learned about her uncle's legacy in Sweetfern Harbor, the more she wondered how the townspeople would fare in his absence. Who else would stand up to the powerful yet unseen

Lady Pendleton who belittled the townspeople with such ease?

As their steps brought them to the end of Main Street, all heads suddenly turned toward a sleek black Cadillac. A woman with dark red hair framing a pair of sharp emerald eyes steered the Cadillac down the street. She threw one disdainful glance out the window. She had a narrow, upturned nose and thin lips with lipstick as red as her hair. As she drove past, she rested her eyes briefly on Phyllis Lindsey.

"I take it that is Lady Pendleton," said Brenda, as Phyllis picked up her pace without a word.

"The one and only," said Carrie, as they hurried to catch up to the housekeeper.

Later that afternoon, Brenda was in her sitting room preparing for her meeting with the banker whom her late Uncle Randolph had retained for years. The appointment was set for the next morning. Having inherited Sheffield Bed and Breakfast, she was thankful she didn't have to worry about being run off the premises by Lady Pendleton, but she was perplexed at the reasoning behind the woman's ongoing actions against the townspeople.

Brenda had not spoken to Edward Graham since finalizing the ownership deed to Sheffield Bed and Breakfast, and as she gathered her thoughts, she wondered about the man and how he dealt with Sweetfern Harbor. She had found him to be professional and knowledgeable and his son Pete seemed universally liked in town. How did he manage to work with Lady Pendleton, who held such animosity toward everyone around her?

That evening when dessert was served in the sitting room

for guests, Brenda pulled Phyllis aside. "Does Edward Graham have a dual personality?"

Phyllis laughed, setting down a lemon chiffon pie and a tray of miniature blueberry tarts. "If you mean, does he act one way around the rest of us and another way around Lady Pendleton, the answer is yes, he does. I feel sorry for Edward. He's caught in a bad place. Everyone tries to excuse him because he has to make a living, but at the same time, we all wish he would put his efforts on the side of the townspeople. She's a tyrant and she seems to control him as much as she does everyone else."

Phyllis excused herself to tidy up the dining room, and Brenda took a seat on an overstuffed armchair by the window. As she quietly watched the guests mingle over dessert, she made up her mind. Phyllis's words were all Brenda needed for now. Once she completed her meeting with the banker, she would stop at Edward Graham's office. Perhaps, as a newcomer, she could get some answers from him that would help her new friends.

When Brenda came down from her apartment the next morning, brilliant sunbeams scattered light prettily down the wide stairway and through the open rooms of the first floor of the bed and breakfast. As tempting as the breakfasts were in her new home, she was determined not to be late for her meeting with the banker. She had made herself a quick cup of tea in her kitchenette and promised herself she would stop by the kitchen later to ask for a bite to eat if she became too hungry.

Just as she was leaving, she ran into Pete Graham in the hallway of the bed and breakfast. "Good morning, Brenda," he said, holding a white envelope in his hand.

"Hi, Pete. I don't see Carrie around right now," said

Brenda, reaching out to take the letter from him, "but I'll put it on her desk."

Pete jerked his hand back and then gave an apologetic smile. "Sorry, I have instructions to give it directly to Phyllis. I hope you don't mind, but it is for her personally."

"I understand," said Brenda. "I think you'll find her in the dining room clearing the table." Brenda walked out the door, eager to get to her meeting. She thought that perhaps Pete's quirky behavior was another part of this village that she was growing to love more and more each day.

It took an hour to go over everything with the banker, and Brenda left satisfied. She headed for Edward Graham's office, walking along Main Street. In the gentle morning breeze of Sweetfern Harbor, tourists stepped out of Morning Sun with coffees in hand, or sat in benches placed along the sidewalk to enjoy the cool ocean breeze.

She turned the corner onto a side street, where the lawyer's office was located. Edward Graham had chosen a regal, old red-brick building for his law practice. Brenda admired its stately lines and old-fashioned elegance, and tried to picture Lady Pendleton's sleek Cadillac driving up to the curb.

The receptionist stated that Mr. Graham was in a meeting and invited Brenda to sit down and wait for him. She offered Brenda some coffee, but she declined, focused on her task. From her seat in the reception area, voices rose and became suddenly audible through Edward's office door.

She tried not to listen but recognized Pete's voice as he practically shouted, "I don't know how you can continue to represent someone as crooked as she is."

Though Edward's voice was softer, it was clear. "I have my own expenses, Pete. I'm mortgaged to the hilt, and if I fall behind she'll snap up the deed from the bank. My hands are tied. And you know I'm doing my best to stop her from going to a big-city lawyer who might let her wreak more havoc than she is already doing."

It was then Brenda noticed the door was not completely closed. The receptionist noticed it at the same time and quietly got up and closed it tightly. When Pete came out, his face was flushed and he clenched his hands in despair. He nodded tersely at Brenda and left without a word.

By the time Brenda was ushered inside Edward's office, he appeared unruffled. Despite his calm exterior, she felt sorry for the man and didn't want to burden him after his difficult conversation with his son. "Mr. Graham, I just wanted to thank you in person for your help."

This would take more thinking on the subject, she thought. Edward had answered his son's accusations and Brenda felt sure she would get the same answers. Her earlier confidence evaporated. It would not be so simple after all to find a quick solution for her Sweetfern Harbor friends.

"I hope things are going well for you, Brenda," said Edward. "Is there anything else I can do for you in regard to Sheffield Bed and Breakfast?"

"Things are running smoothly," Brenda said, working to keep her smile confident. "Uncle Randolph knew what he was doing when he hired the staff and the financial records are in order. It's been a while since we spoke so I simply wanted to thank you again for your help. I'll leave you now. I'm sure you have plenty of work to do and I should be getting back."

He stood and shook her hand. His smile was pleasant but when Brenda closed the door behind her she noticed his furrowed brow as he peered over papers on his desk.

chapter three

As the hugely popular July boat race approached, Sweetfern Harbor burst into a frenzy of preparation and everyone in town seemed grateful for the distraction from the latest financial troubles. The annual event had grown each year, and this year it seemed that the town overflowed with teams of contestants and spectators crowding the sidewalks and parks.

The Sheffield Bed and Breakfast was filled to capacity, and Brenda was kept busy planning an evening cocktail reception for her guests. After the mayor announced the winner, the oceanfront lawn of the Sheffield would be an ideal location to sip cool drinks and watch the fireworks bursting over the harbor.

At Morning Sun Coffee, amidst the bustle of customers, Molly was instructing Logan Tucker to be on time every morning for the next week. "I need you every minute," said Molly. "By the way, Lady Pendleton is coming to pick up her weekly batch of custom-roasted coffee. I'll get it ready but if I'm not here make sure she gets it."

Logan grinned and nodded. "I remember race week last year, Molly. You can count on me. I'll even make her drink exactly as she likes it." Lady Pendleton always ordered a cappuccino when she came to pick up her weekly order, and had been known to demand a replacement if it did not meet her standards. Molly had to smile. Logan's boyish mannerisms drew customers in, though it seemed to have no real effect on Lady Pendleton.

Molly thought back to an incident she had witnessed just the previous week. William Pendleton always dutifully followed his wife into the coffee shop. He had started to hand Molly a tip as she passed him his wife's packaged order.

"What are you thinking, William?" said his wife with an accusing look. "You're too soft. Tips should be earned for real service."

Molly was chagrined to hear this. William's eyes held sympathy for Molly but he did as his wife told him and stuffed the folded bills back into his pants pocket. Molly gave William a sympathetic shrug. He picked up the packaged coffee beans and followed his wife out.

Thinking back to Lady Pendleton's dismissive manner, Molly could only cross her fingers that Logan's charm would hold out for the day. The shop was so busy she would barely have time to think, let alone supervise Logan when the Pendletons came in.

Crowds swarmed the town and excitement grew to a high pitch as the race was due to begin. Everyone headed down to the beach with binoculars. The more elite spectators were watching from inside an air-conditioned building on the waterfront with massive glass windows that looked out over the harbor. Box seats filled and everyone there had a spectacular view of the water. Brenda watched the race from the lawn with her guests and the staff of the Sheffield Bed and Breakfast, with a newfound appreciation for how beautiful her new town could be when it put on a show for visitors.

At the cocktail reception that evening, Brenda was pleased to see how beautiful the Sheffield looked in the pale July twilight. On the lawn there were clusters of guests and townspeople who had dropped by to celebrate, and everyone raved about the sparkling pink lemonade Phyllis made especially for the party.

Brenda stopped at the refreshments table set under the rose arbor to breathe in the perfume of a gorgeous arrangement of blooms that Jenny Rivers had provided for the party. Little lights twinkled from the trees and the effect was breathtaking.

Phyllis walked up and smiled at her, holding out a tempting platter of treats.

"Oh, Phyllis. Everything looks perfect."

Her housekeeper nodded with satisfaction. "This is Sheffield House in all her glory! I'm glad you're enjoying yourself."

They each nibbled on the small tea cakes from Sweet Treats Bakery until finally Brenda laughed, saying, "Phyllis, I'm going to have to sit on my hands or I will eat them all!" After some well-earned levity, Brenda could see that despite her mirth, there was a sadness lingering around Phyllis, and she pleaded with her housekeeper to unburden herself.

"It's Jenny Rivers, I just can't stop thinking about her. She is getting desperate. She can't afford to lose her florist shop. She is young and just starting out in life."

Brenda nodded in sympathy. "I wish I could just give her the money the way my uncle would have, once upon a time, but the Sheffield fortune isn't what it used to be, as wonderful as this place is. But perhaps...I do have an idea that might help her. Is she still here tonight? Maybe you can send her my way if you see her."

"That is a splendid idea, Brenda. I'll get right on that."

It wasn't long before Jenny Rivers sought Brenda out, with a curious look in her eyes. Brenda was pleased to finally pass along her advice. "Jenny, I know this lawsuit is hanging over your head. But I've heard that if a law firm thinks you have a good case, they might even help you sue Lady Pendleton without you having to pay a cent. The lawyer's fee would just come out of whatever money you get in the settlement."

"I can't believe my ears. That would be the answer to my prayers! Thank you, Brenda. I'm so touched that you thought of me and the trouble with my little flower shop." She smiled in gratitude, and Brenda was satisfied to finally give back to this wonderful little town that had won her over. But Jenny wasn't done. "By the way, did you know that my dad is a detective like you? You'd have a lot in common with him. And he's single." Brenda stared at her.

Jenny dimpled and pointed discreetly to a tall man standing near the refreshments table, some distance away from where the two women stood. "That's him. Mac, my dad. He's been widowed a long time. My mother passed away ten years ago and he never remarried."

Brenda struggled to gather her thoughts. "First of all, thank you for the offer, but I was not a detective per se. I take it he's with the police force here?"

Jenny nodded her head. She liked Brenda Sheffield and knew her father was lonely when not in the middle of a case. "I know you worked some crime cases, Brenda," said Jenny. "I heard you were good at what you did."

Brenda laughed. "My boss never gave me a lot of credit, but I did help solve a few of his cases. I liked delving into crime cases. I'm sure your dad is a great person, but I'm just not interested in meeting anyone right now."

"I didn't say you had to marry him," Jenny teased back. "He would be someone to hang out with and share interests."

Brenda blushed. "I'll think about it. In the meantime, do you have a good law firm in mind?"

"I asked my dad about that. He is making inquiries for

me. Thank you again for your help." As the two women made chitchat, Brenda was relieved to have steered the conversation away from her romantic prospects. She couldn't help but notice Mac Rivers look her way once or twice, but she had to admit it was hard to pay attention to anything but the brilliant display of fireworks bursting over the harbor as the night came to a splendid conclusion.

Sweetfern Harbor finally settled back into its normal summer routine once the boat race gala was over. Brenda felt more and more at ease in her new career. She loved meeting new people and chatting with her guests. All had fascinating stories to tell and she hung on to their every word. As the last guests from the boat race checked out, Sheffield House was shined and polished until it gleamed, every member of the staff working their hardest to get ready for the new guests that would arrive soon.

"I'm going to cut some flowers for my room," said Brenda, heading out to the front garden with a pair of shears and her gardening gloves. She had never been much of a green thumb but since the groundskeeper took care of the details, she enjoyed wandering amidst the roses, peonies, and irises planted in the garden of the grand mansion. She liked nothing better than to wake up each morning to the scent of the ocean breeze and a fresh-picked bouquet from her own garden.

Just as she bent to cut a deep fuchsia peony, she heard the screeching sound of tires taking a corner too fast. It was such an unaccustomed sound for the small, sedate town that at first, she couldn't believe her ears. She watched an unmistakable sleek Cadillac tearing up the road toward the bed and breakfast.

To date, Lady Pendleton had not visited Sheffield Bed and Breakfast. She wondered why the arrogant redheaded woman raced so recklessly toward her establishment today, of all days. The Cadillac's brakes slammed on with a squeal and the car's front left wheel landed on the curb in front of the house. The ignition went quiet. Brenda waited for Lady Pendleton to emerge but nothing happened.

"I may as well get this meeting over with," Brenda sighed to no one in particular.

She walked down the steps from the garden to the sidewalk to investigate, but when she came within view of the luxury car, she stepped back quickly. This was no social call.

Lady Pendleton was bent over the steering wheel in the driver's seat at a strange angle. Her red hair, pulled back in a taut chignon, glimmered dully in the sunlight that shone through the open window.

"Lady Pendleton, are you all right?" asked Brenda in alarm. There was no answer. Brenda shook her thin shoulder to rouse her. "Are you ill?" When Lady Pendleton still did not respond, Brenda realized she was unconscious. Her heart beating fast with suppressed panic, she reached for the cell phone in her pocket and dialed 911.

Within minutes, sirens could be heard heading toward Sheffield Bed and Breakfast. The ambulance was first to arrive, followed by a squad car. Brenda stood back and watched as two paramedics wheeled a gurney over to the car and quickly worked to extract the limp form. The street and sidewalk in front of the Sheffield was quickly swarming with people as several other emergency vehicles quickly surrounded the scene. Brenda could clearly see Lady Pendleton's motionless chest as the paramedics applied an oxygen mask and started performing CPR. When a white van drove up and several people climbed out in uniform jackets labeled "County Coroner," Brenda's suspicions were sadly confirmed. The paramedics pronounced the town's affluent tyrant dead at the scene.

By this time, cordons had been placed to block the cars and people coming up from Main Street. Later, Brenda learned that shop owners locked up and hurried to the scene. It was as if everyone had to see for themselves that the most despised member of Sweetfern Harbor was truly dead. There was a stir as the crowd parted and the police let Dr. Thomas Windham through. Brenda watched as he examined Lady Pendleton, seemed to shake his head sadly, and then sign some paperwork for the County Coroner's office. A murmur went through the crowd as tourists and Sweetfern Harbor residents alike watched as the body was zipped into a bag and carefully loaded into the county van.

In all the commotion, Brenda had hardly noticed Phyllis and Carrie, who had come to stand with her in mutual shock and support. They watched as a younger officer strung yellow caution tape around the scene and another started to order the crowd of onlookers to disperse.

Brenda could see Detective Rivers kneeling by the open door of the Cadillac as he inspected its interior. He was standing right where she had been standing when she had seen Lady Pendleton's strangely crumpled form—she shook her head to clear her mind of the horrible memory.

"This has to be Mac Rivers's biggest case ever," said Carrie. "I wonder what caused her death. It wasn't a crash, she just stopped right there at the curb, right Brenda?"

Brenda nodded. "I wonder why she was driving like a maniac," said Brenda. "I thought she was going to keep going right onto the lawn and into the garden. Maybe she had a heart attack or a stroke and couldn't control the car," Brenda mused.

Detective Rivers was conferring with one of the

paramedics who pointed toward Brenda. The detective nodded and walked over to her. He introduced himself and asked if she was the one who discovered Lady Pendleton slumped over the steering wheel.

As strange as the situation was, Brenda could barely answer, "Yes" to his inquiry. She was mesmerized by his good looks and stunned to be meeting him face to face like this. I should have said hello at the cocktail reception, she thought.

He appeared to be in his early forties or so and his thick blond hair lifted slightly in the light wind. Brenda realized he had asked her something but she had no idea what.

"I'm sorry," she said helplessly. "What did you say?"

"I said I'd like to speak to you privately in a few minutes. Are you willing to give me a statement with more details?"

Brenda felt her cheeks warm up. "I'm available whenever you are." She bit her tongue as she heard the double meaning in her words too late to take it back. What was wrong with her? His looks and his strong, assured confidence were completely disarming her. She noted a slight curve to his mouth when he saw her blush and she looked down, flustered. Messages were being sent and received that had nothing to do with the dead Lady Pendleton.

Sometime later, she waited in the library of the bed and breakfast, trying and failing to contain her boredom. She had been told it might be a while before the detective was free to meet with her, since documenting and clearing away the crime scene could take several hours. The library was a beautifully wood-paneled room with floor-to-ceiling bookshelves stocked with her late uncle's collection of leather-bound classics as well as an excellent selection of contemporary novels. She had picked up a book that looked promising enough, but instead found herself staring out the window thinking back to Detective Rivers and his sly grin.

A knock at the library doors startled her out of her thoughts. It was Carrie, finally bringing the news that he was ready to talk with her. When the detective came in, she offered him a seat in one of the tufted leather armchairs, then turned to close the doors for privacy. With her back turned momentarily, she willed herself not to say anything silly.

She sat down across from him as he took out a notebook and pencil.

"Tell me everything you noticed, in detail," he said.

She took a breath. "I was in the garden when I heard her tires squealing. At first, I couldn't figure out why she was driving in such a crazy way. I suppose she didn't realize it. At least, she braked and turned the ignition off rather than crashing." Brenda continued with the scant details of what she had seen before the paramedics had arrived. "Do you know how she died, Detective Rivers?"

"Please, call me Mac," he said with a polite but warm smile. "Everyone else in town does. It is too early to determine cause of death, but her husband agreed right away to an autopsy. We should have results soon. She's a little young for a heart attack, according to Dr. Windham. Of course, that is just his first impression." He shifted in the chair. "How do you like our little village?"

"I have been surprised at how friendly everyone has been. I am happy here and am getting the hang of running a bed and breakfast, which I love. I've met your daughter, Jenny. She is lovely and so friendly. I love her flower shop—she did some amazing arrangements for the cocktail party we had in July."

"I'm proud of the way she has lived her life. It was hard when her mother passed away, Jenny was so young then. But we've both had to move forward." He stood to go. "I'll probably have more questions for you as they come up. Jenny told me you worked with a private investigator back in Michigan? She said you solved cases. I may need to call on you for some insight if you don't mind."

Brenda smiled, trying not to blush again in

embarrassment. "I've tried to tell people I was an assistant to the PI. I did help him break a few cases and found it all very intriguing. I admit...I've always wanted to get into the business, myself." She tried to sound nonchalant as he gave her an appraising, intrigued look. "This is probably Sweetfern Harbor's biggest case, isn't it?"

He chuckled. "By far. Brenda, thank you for your statement. I've got to get back to the station now, but I'll be in touch", he said, standing to go.

"Anytime," Brenda said, hoping she didn't sound too eager. She showed the detective to the front door of Sheffield Bed and Breakfast.

Phyllis hurried over to Brenda as she closed the front door. "What does he think happened? Everyone is so happy she is dead and gone." Phyllis's hand flew to her mouth. "I guess I shouldn't say that, but it is hard to feel bad about her death."

"They don't know anything yet," said Brenda, watching Mac through the window as he climbed into his car and drove away. "But don't apologize for saying it. She won't be missed, after all."

Phyllis stood next to her. Only one police car remained at the scene, as an officer took down the yellow caution tape. A tow truck had long since taken away the sleek Cadillac. "We saw them put things in a bag. I wonder what they found in her car."

Brenda shook her head. In a town like Sweetfern Harbor, she knew for certain that if anyone knew anything, it wouldn't be long before the news was passed along.

As Detective Rivers drove off from Sheffield Bed and Breakfast he thought about all the people who deeply resented Lady Pendleton. If this were a normal case, the first step would be to investigate anyone with a probable cause or a grudge against the deceased. How on earth would he manage a case of this scope? They would have to interview practically the entire town. The more he thought about it, the more he realized Brenda Sheffield might be his ace in the hole.

Back at the station, he passed by the front desk and went to the office he shared with Tim Donnelly, the other detective on the force. Together, they covered the whole county and had never seen a crime of this magnitude.

"I bagged a few loose items from the Cadillac, as you asked," said Tim, looking up as Mac walked in. "Just some random things. Otherwise, the car was immaculate."

Tim sat down at his desk and pulled on a pair of gloves. The first item Tim pulled out was a green leather appointment book with gold-edged paper. Leafing through it carefully to the current month, he could see the court date for her lawsuit against Jenny Rivers, and in a Notes column was a brief list of names marked "To Discuss." Mac grimaced to realize this list looked like she was on a mission to harass everyone in town. He was most uncomfortable to see his daughter's name scrawled there in Lady Pendleton's heavy cursive. Next, Tim handed him a small brocade purse that held nothing of real interest, just a driver's license, checkbook, and credit cards.

"What's that envelope?"

"That's the most interesting find of all," replied Tim with a rueful smile, reaching in carefully to retrieve an envelope that had clearly been opened, its flap ripped jaggedly as if opened in great haste. He passed it to Mac. "It's addressed to Phyllis Lindsey." Mac examined the envelope closely, seeing that it was crumpled as if someone had balled it up in anger. "I didn't take the letter out yet so you get the pleasure, Detective."

Mac took the letter out and unfolded it. As his eyes scanned the words, his mouth fell open and he had to read the signature twice to make sure he read it correctly. He looked up at Tim in a daze. "The letter isn't from Lady Pendleton, it's from her husband William. Apparently, he was in love with Phyllis Lindsey. They had been meeting in secret. Apparently, his wife discovered this letter before it reached its destination."

The two detectives stared at the letter. Tim laid it down on the desk as if it would explode.

"Well," said Tim, clearing his throat uncertainly. "This certainly adds a new wrinkle to things."

"I'll say. You put together the list of interviewees in order of importance. I have to go pay William Pendleton a visit." As he headed for the old Pendleton home on the sloping hill that overlooked Sweetfern Harbor, Mac Rivers began to wonder what other secrets might be hiding under the surface of the sleepy village.

An hour later, Mac climbed back into his car and watched the afternoon sun sparkling on the harbor and the ocean beyond. He dialed Tim and placed the call on speakerphone.

"Donnelly, it's Rivers. William Pendleton is in shock, poor guy, but I don't think he had anything to do with her death. He was so shaken, I offered to fetch Phyllis in my car to keep him company. I've never seen a man fall over himself in embarrassment like that. He couldn't believe I'd seen the letter."

"Did he have anything helpful to say?"

"Not really. His gardener vouched for him being home all day."

"Not really surprising. Poor fella. Rivers, this list of interviewees is getting longer than my arm. It might be faster to get the whole town roster, if you know what I mean. You know how she was with real estate around here."

"I know," said Mac, his jaw tightening a little as he thought of his daughter's name scrawled in that appointment book.

"How are we going to handle this? It's too much work."

"Don't worry, I think I have a plan," said the detective, and they hung up. As his car swept down the hill toward the station, he thought perhaps he might be back at the Sheffield Bed and Breakfast sooner than he thought.

A few days later, the town newspaper published a story about the death of Priscilla Pendleton. No one had to read the printed word, however copies of the paper were snatched up all over town as souvenirs. Rumors spread like wildfire that Lady Pendleton had been poisoned, but even Pete Graham wasn't able to pin down whether it was fact or fiction when Brenda pressed him about it.

"Poison does seem like poetic justice," said Carrie. "Maybe that husband of hers decided he'd finally had enough of her.

"William Pendleton is a sweet-natured man and would never do something like that. Besides, he had put up with her all of these years, why would he decide to poison her now?" Phyllis spoke in a voice filled with agitation.

Brenda recalled the soft curve of her mouth when William's name was mentioned once before in a casual conversation. She shook her head. Phyllis had been oddly quiet ever since Lady Pendleton's death.

The three women sipped at their tea, tucked into snug armchairs in the sitting room at the end of a long day. "Maybe you're right," said Carrie, chagrined by Phyllis's response. "Can you believe her name was Priscilla? It's too perfect," she giggled, changing the subject.

Something else came to Brenda's mind suddenly: the day she had run into Pete Graham hand-delivering a letter to Phyllis. Could it have been from William Pendleton? Brenda almost had to laugh at herself for the notion. It all sounded silly and implausible.

But still, someone knew something. Someone in town was keeping a secret. Brenda decided to do what she did best: pay close attention to everyone and see whose secrets might come tumbling out in the wake of the death of the town's tyrant.

chapter four

It was hard for Brenda to get comfortable in bed that night. She tossed and turned until she finally got up and made a cup of chamomile tea. She sat by the window overlooking the gardens. Moonlight cast a muted haze over dewy grass and flowers. Ordinarily, this dreamy landscape would have caught her interest, but her thoughts flowed to the bizarre events of the last few days.

Just that afternoon, Detective Mac Rivers had called the Sheffield Bed and Breakfast, asking to meet with her again. A little butterfly of nervousness fluttered in her stomach when she thought of seeing him again, but she tried to firmly put that out of her mind. It was far more important to start a little detective work of her own. Brenda grabbed her notebook and a pen.

She put William Pendleton at the top of her list. Next was Jenny Rivers. Jenny was distraught about the impending loss of her business due to the lawsuit Lady Pendleton filed against her. She wrote down Pete Graham, wondering what he knew about that mysterious hand-carried letter. The letter was for Phyllis, did that mean her own housekeeper was also a suspect?

As she continued making her list, she thought back to

each and every person in town who had said something had to be done about Lady Pendleton. She put her pen down and leaned back in her chair. Everyone was a suspect.

These thoughts tormented her a little longer until the chamomile tea kicked in, and then she went back to bed. Gazing at the moonbeams as her eyes drooped shut, Brenda sleepily promised herself she would make some headway in this mess during her meeting the next morning with Detective Rivers.

After a light breakfast the next morning, Brenda returned to her apartment to check her makeup. She swept on a little powder with a soft brush and then dabbed some concealer on the dark circles under her eyes from lack of sleep. She inspected her reflection in the mirror and grabbed her notebook.

As she headed down the stairs, Mac Rivers was just entering the foyer. He looked up to greet her with a smile that made the corners of his eyes crinkle good-naturedly, his blond hair combed back neatly.

"Miss Sheffield," he said.

"Please, call me Brenda," she said, nodding professionally. "Do you mind if we go out to the garden to talk? It's too nice to stay indoors this morning."

"Not at all, lead the way," he replied. They walked around the side of the bed and breakfast, following the pathway to the backyard. Brenda sat on the pine bench at the edge of the rose garden and took a deep breath of the sweetly scented air. She hoped his questions for her would go quickly. She had her own observations about the townspeople she wanted to share with him.

"I want you to tell me again exactly what happened once

you saw Lady Pendleton's car careening down the street," he said, pen and notebook in hand.

Brenda repeated what she remembered and tried to include any helpful details. He appeared satisfied with her answers. She hadn't changed her story, after all, and was more of a bystander. "I'm sure you've guessed at the scope of our investigation by now," he said. "From what the doc told us…well, we're going on the assumption it was poison. I wonder if you have any thoughts about who could have killed her?" he asked.

Brenda eagerly opened her notebook and went down the first few names on her list, quickly running through her observations on each person. She skipped over Jenny, but he was savvy and said, "What about my daughter? Isn't she on your list? Lady Pendleton had filed a lawsuit against Jenny. We should get everything out in the open or we won't be able to work together very well."

"I have her on the list," Brenda admitted, "but knowing her, I don't believe she had anything to do with it. It's not as if she serves food or drink at Blossoms. How would she have poisoned her?"

Mac breathed deeply. "I am glad you see it that way. I am sure my daughter had nothing to do with it but I had to get your honest take on her." They moved on to William Pendleton. "We found a letter written by William to your housekeeper. It was in the car with Lady Pendleton. Did you know they were secretly exchanging letters?"

Brenda was intrigued, and told him about the incident with the letter Pete Graham brought to Phyllis. "He insisted it had to be hand-delivered to her. I didn't think much of it at the time. It's the only time I saw Pete with a letter like that. Phyllis hasn't said anything about secret meetings with Mr. Pendleton, but I'm not sure she would tell me. I don't pry into the personal lives of my employees. I think Phyllis prefers it that way."

She thought for a moment back to that heart-racing moment when the Cadillac had been barreling down the street toward the bed and breakfast. "Lady Pendleton must have been rushing here to confront Phyllis," said Brenda.

"That's what I've concluded, too," said Mac. "I'll be honest, Brenda. We have so many interviews to wade through, but what I really need is someone like you— someone who can see people for who they really are. Someone who hasn't been steeped in town gossip for decades. Someone who makes friends in a way that a detective can't," he finished with an apologetic smile.

Brenda nodded eagerly in agreement. "I want to help any way I can. If we concentrate on businesses who served food or drink to Lady Pendleton, we could narrow your interview list a little bit. I can follow up after your official questioning and then we can compare notes afterward."

Mac readily agreed, and they went through the list of businesses that served food and drink in town. There were no clues yet, and certainly no one in this seaside town who fit the personality of a murderer. But it was somewhere to start.

Mac stood up and thanked Brenda for her help.

"I have to get back to the station. In the meantime, keep your eyes and ears open."

After she watched him walk down the path and leave the garden, Brenda felt a familiar mix of excitement and nerves tumble through her. She was sure she would have plenty of opportunity to observe reactions since there was only one topic of conversation in town.

She went back inside through the delivery entrance and through the kitchen door saw Phyllis talking softly to the chef. When they turned to see who had entered, Phyllis quickly turned away, but not fast enough that Brenda didn't note her reddened eyes and tear-streaked face.

A half hour later, she answered a soft knock on her apartment door. It was Phyllis.

"I feel I should explain the breakdown you witnessed downstairs earlier. It's just that William—Mr. Pendleton has been brought in twice now for questions about Lady Pendleton's murder." She sniffled quietly and pulled a tissue from her skirt pocket. "I know he would never hurt anyone. He lived with his wife for years and they had their separate interests and did just fine."

Brenda waited as Phyllis started to speak and then stopped herself, struggling.

Then, the housekeeper sighed and said, "He just isn't the kind of person who could have done something like that."

"How do you know for sure?"

Phyllis sat down across from Brenda and wiped her eyes again. "I will tell you something you may not be aware of. We managed to keep it a secret from everyone. William and I are in love with one another." When she finished saying this and looked up to meet Brenda's eyes, she was taken aback to see understanding, not shock, plainly written on her employer's face. "I suppose since you are a sleuth in your own right that you already knew that. Does everyone know my secret?"

"No, I promise you," Brenda reassured her. "I wondered ever since I saw Pete insist on personally delivering a letter to you. I didn't give much thought to it at the time, but was it a letter from William?"

Phyllis nodded her head. Brenda had no intention of telling her of the letter found in the Cadillac. That was something Mac would divulge in good time.

"I've been asked to visit the police station, Mac wants to question me. Do you think I should tell him about my relationship with William?"

"I think you should tell him everything that would be helpful to the case," replied Brenda carefully. "Why take the risk? My old boss used to say that people always reveal more by what they conceal, even if it's something minor. The sooner you can clear yourself the better."

"It's not just our relationship," said Phyllis, taking a shaky breath. "William told me about something that happened." Brenda leaned forward, intrigued. "Just a few days ago, his wife found something out. Not everything, but she suspected something was up and confronted William. He tried to tell her she was crazy and to respect his privacy, but she just kept pushing and pushing. He said—he said he flew into a rage. He just couldn't take it anymore. He lost it." Phyllis looked up, wiping away her tears again. "He said she was so shocked by it that she finally left him alone. He'd never done that before."

Brenda contemplated this for a moment. It certainly seemed to be a new side of William, but it was far from a smoking gun. "The truth will set you free, Phyllis. That's all that matters."

Phyllis nodded and took a deep breath. "I feel so much better now that I've told you, Brenda. I'll be honest and upfront with the detective."

After Phyllis left, Brenda reflected on their conversation and became convinced that the housekeeper knew nothing about the murder of Lady Pendleton. She was not concerned for herself, she just wanted to protect William. Whether he was truly innocent, time would tell. As far as what she had promised Detective Rivers, she listened to her gut and knew that Phyllis couldn't be a suspect. She vowed to get in touch with Mac the next day to tell him about the confrontation between Lady Pendleton and her husband.

The next day proved to be a cloudy one. The sun attempted to break through the clouds, but didn't manage it. Despite the gloomy morning weather, Brenda asked Phyllis to take a walk with her to Morning Sun Coffee. It would be good to see

Molly and she hoped for Phyllis's sake that some of the gossip about Lady Pendleton's death had died down.

Phyllis perked up at her offer and went to grab a lightweight sweater. Brenda did the same. The ocean breeze felt much cooler with no sun.

When they entered the Morning Sun, Logan was behind the counter taking orders. Molly came out from the kitchen and her eyes lit up. She waved to Phyllis and Brenda as they sat down at a window side table. A couple of minutes later she brought them coffees and a plate of miniature cinnamon rolls and sat down to chat with them.

"I hear Jenny is in a lot of trouble," Molly said.

"I thought all the lawsuits were dropped," said Phyllis, taking a sip of her steaming hot coffee.

"Lawsuits have been dropped, but word is that Jenny is still at the top of the suspect list."

Phyllis's mouth dropped open. She slowly put the small roll back on the plate. Brenda stared at Molly. "Why is she at the top of the list?" She wondered why Mac had not said anything about this to her during their earlier meeting.

"Someone has been hinting around town that she was more than a little angry with Lady Pendleton over the rent raise."

"But that's true of everyone in town," Phyllis pointed out.

"That's true, but Jenny also had the lawsuit hanging over her head. Jenny complained to everyone and kept saying she was "going to do something" about the woman. Those are her words. I don't believe Jenny did it at all. She was mad enough, but so were a lot of people around here."

Just then, Pete Graham came into the shop. He handed Molly her mail and gratefully accepted her offer of a cup of hot coffee. "Jenny Rivers is distraught. She closed Blossoms today and left," he said. "She isn't answering her phone. Hope just went to go to Mac's house to see if she is there. I think she ran away because she is being accused of killing Lady Pendleton." He waited for a response from the women, but everyone was in shock to hear of such a reaction from someone they thought they knew so well.

"Pete, what do you make of this? Why are they going after Jenny? Everyone threatened to do something about Lady Pendleton. Idle threats don't make her guilty of murder." Phyllis's eyes lit with an indignant anger rarely seen in the housekeeper. "I'm surprised at you, Pete Graham, for passing judgment on Jenny like that. You shouldn't spread these kinds of rumors when there's an investigation going on," she finished, her motherly brows knit in a stern reprimand.

"I'm just telling you what's going around. I'm sorry. I know she is a good friend of yours and I didn't mean anything by it." He looked from Phyllis to Molly to Brenda, as if searching for a sympathetic face.

Brenda couldn't meet his eyes and just listened. "Stop that rumor right here, Pete. The town doesn't need to start turning against one another," said Molly firmly, patting her mother's arm to calm her.

Pete flushed to hear these words from his girlfriend. "I—Molly...I'll—" he seemed lost for words for a moment as he searched her face and read the anguish written there as she comforted her mother. "I'll do better," he said finally, duly ashamed and agreeing to squelch the rumor.

William Pendleton quickened his steps across the marble floors of the ornate house, feeling a new sense of purpose. After the initial shock of his conversation with Detective Rivers had worn off, he had awoken the next day to find himself energetic and, for the first time, the master of his own domain.

He had quickly settled on the necessary details—after the body was released by the coroner, there would be no formal funeral or memorial, simply cremation and an unadorned urn in the family mausoleum. The cremation services director had inquired about placing an obituary in the newspaper, and after a moment's thought, William had simply declined. Then it would be finished.

The peaceful quiet in the house was a balm to him. No arrogant voice ringing out as she berated the staff. No incessant clicking of heels along the marble hallway as she stalked up and down on one of her tirades.

As he walked toward the kitchen, he found his lips curving in a smile. No longer would he have to live under the thumb of his dismal wife and hide his true love, Phyllis Lindsey. Pete Graham, long paid handsomely for his discretion, would no longer be necessary.

For the first time in a long time William Pendleton breathed deeply. In the kitchen, he found John, the longtime butler to the Pendleton house, reviewing some papers with the chef.

"John," he said, with an easy smile. "I think I'd like my old chair brought up from the basement storage room. It was…unfairly sent down there some years ago on the orders of Mrs. Pendleton. I think you remember the one?"

"The brown leather easy chair, sir?"

"Precisely. I know right where I want it to go," he said, and knew exactly the cigar he wanted to retrieve from his humidor to celebrate this wonderful day.

That night, after Morning Sun Coffee's last customer had left, Molly Lindsey and Logan Tucker wiped the tables and then sat down to enjoy sandwiches and iced tea. The day had been a busy one. It seemed to be not just tourists in town, but people who had come to gawk and gossip about Sweetfern Harbor's crime of the century.

"I'm glad she isn't around to harass any of us any longer," said Molly. "Most of all, I'm happy not to have to pay an arm and a leg to import those special coffee beans she demanded."

"Yeah," said Logan, taking a long sip of his iced tea. "I hated it when she came in here. She never failed to put me down every chance she got." Molly raised her eyebrows to hear this. "The last time she came in here, she implied I was a failure for working here instead of doing 'something better' with my life. I don't know what she was getting at. I like working here and you pay me enough so I can take Carrie out every Saturday night." He grinned at his boss. "I'm glad the wicked witch is dead. Poison is fitting since she spent her life poisoning every one of us."

Molly noted that behind his humor, a flash of anger crossed Logan's face. They finished their sandwiches in comfortable silence until Logan stood up and stretched.

"I'll lock up, Logan, you go home and get some rest," said Molly.

Logan couldn't stop the yawn that overcame him. "Thanks, boss. Have a good night."

Carrie Martin went into the bed and breakfast office and sat down to answer emails with dates of availability. Her mind wandered as she automatically typed and answered the queries, thinking back to Randolph Sheffield and how many times he had tried to meet with Lady Pendleton privately to reason with her on behalf of the townspeople. It was to no avail, but Mr. Sheffield had never given up the cause, as busy as he was.

"All the money in the world won't cure her bitter heart," he had said sadly upon his return from one of these attempts. "She is coldhearted and that's all there is to it."

At one time, Mr. Sheffield had even tried a different

approach, offering to buy some land from Lady Pendleton at a premium, hoping that the families who lived in the houses there could enjoy peace and reasonable rents if he was the owner. Lady Pendleton had refused to even consider his offer.

Rebuffed in his real estate offer and witnessing how her greed threatened Sweetfern Harbor, Mr. Sheffield had found other ways to work his will. He helped Holly Williams get the funding to start her bakery so she could be the supplier to his bed and breakfast, and Jenny Rivers had started out her florist business with a handshake agreement from the older gentleman promising her a steady stream of business supplying lavish floral arrangements for the events at his establishment. He had touched nearly every shopkeeper or business in town, making the Sheffield Bed and Breakfast the instrument of his benevolence when he couldn't fix the problem of Lady Pendleton directly.

Pressing send on the last email in the batch, Carrie swiveled around in her chair and smiled. At last, Randolph, she said to herself, Lady Pendleton has her final reward. If only you could see!

Carrie heard Brenda coming down the stairs. She liked her new boss but no one could ever replace Randolph Sheffield. Luckily, the community of friendly, close-knit families and businesses in Sweetfern Harbor would outlast any boss. That was Mr. Sheffield's true legacy.

Brenda waved to Carrie from the doorway.

"It's been a busy day, Carrie," said Brenda, reaching for the phone on the desk and dialing Mac Rivers. "Detective? It's me, Brenda." Carrie was surprised to see her boss's cheeks turn a very pretty shade of pink as she arranged to meet the detective at the police station that afternoon.

Brenda hung up the phone and turned to leave. "I'll be back later. Don't forget to take that deposit to the bank," she reminded Carrie.

"Don't worry, Brenda. You take all the time with Detective Rivers that you need," Carrie replied a little cheekily.

From where she sat, she watched Brenda walk into the hall and stop at the hallway mirror to smooth her hair into place. She couldn't help but notice that the blush did not fade from Brenda's cheeks as she turned to go and stepped out into the brilliant summer light.

chapter five

When Brenda arrived at the detective's office promptly at three that afternoon, Mac Rivers greeted her with a warm smile. "Come in, have a seat," he said, offering her a chair. "As you can see, we're just getting started," he said and gestured to the mess of paper and files covering his desk.

"I'm happy to help, Detective," replied Brenda, looking around at the various lists and pictures that he had pinned up behind his desk. There was a map of the town there.

"I have tried to retrace Lady Pendleton's activities the day of her death," said Mac, looking up at the map and gesturing to the pins and markings all over it. "The coroner's report confirmed that she ingested a poisonous substance, so we are still following every lead about where she might have eaten or drunk."

He turned back to face Brenda and ran a hand through his hair as he flipped through a file. "We're looking into her husband's activities that day, too."

"I called you because I learned something from Phyllis that you need to know. Lady Pendleton had her suspicions about William's secret relationship," said Brenda. "Everyone knew theirs wasn't a happy marriage, but I guess her suspicions drove her out of her mind. She ranted and raved at him but had no proof. William lost his cool for the first time, according to Phyllis. And in a big way." Mac's eyes bore deeply into Brenda's as he listened. "Only then would she leave William alone. I'm not sure if William isn't a man of surprising depths—not just love but perhaps hatred as well."

"Well, that fits with my pieces of the puzzle. William didn't say anything about that fight, but he said she snatched a letter out of Pete Graham's hands that morning. According to William," said Mac, scanning a witness statement in his hands, "she read the letter and stalked to her car with it still in her hand. William wasn't very forthcoming about its contents but we now know it was a love letter to Phyllis. She sped from the driveway at a murderous speed, according to William, and Pete said the same in a separate interview."

"So she was coming to confront Phyllis," finished Brenda. "Maybe she would have killed William in a rage afterward, too, if the poison hadn't stopped her first. When did she ingest it?"

"He's not sure whether it was a one-time dose, or over a longer period of time. I'm dismissing William as a suspect. Things were normal between them, except for that fight and the letter Lady Pendleton took from Pete. It was an ordinary day and he had no idea she was going to threaten Phyllis like that." Mac folded his arms on the desk and shifted forward. "I'm sure William did not poison his wife. He never cooked for her. There is a chef in the house who has been with them for the past twenty years. I interviewed the chef, too, and he's clear. So is the rest of their staff. We searched the Pendleton home and did not find any poison, or traces of poison."

There was a moment as they both contemplated this.

"I heard your daughter has become a prime suspect," said Brenda carefully. She watched Mac's expression closely. He closed his eyes tightly.

"Jenny met with Lady Pendleton in the flower shop the day before her death. Jenny had the usual rent check ready for her. But it wasn't enough because, without any warning, Lady Pendleton told her she had to pay for a complete redo of the shop's plumbing or else she would file a lawsuit. She said because Jenny had caused the plumbing problems—who knows if that's the truth but I doubt it—she'd broken the lease and so she was increasing the rent, too. Jenny was devastated and tried to stand up to her. You can't just spring a demand like that on someone, she didn't have more money to give her." He wiped his forehead with the back of his hand. "Lady Pendleton then demanded an expensive bouquet and said that would take care of the increase this month, but she expected to be paid in full the next month. And she said to expect the lawsuit over the plumbing costs immediately."

"That all sounds sad, but it doesn't make Jenny sound guilty. Why is she a prime suspect?"

"She was so mad about it all that she told her best friends Molly Lindsey and Holly Williams what happened. She also closed her shop and stormed over to Edward Graham's office. She demanded he do something about his client or she would do something drastic. Of course, she didn't mean anything by it, but Edward probably mentioned the encounter to his son Pete, and we all know telling Pete Graham anything means it's public knowledge." He wiped his brow again.

"How are you holding up, Detective?" Brenda's brow was furrowed and Mac cast her a sudden, grateful look.

"Chief Ingram told me this morning that there will be more scrutiny of Jenny but for me not to interview her since she is my daughter." His shoulders slumped. "I know Jenny would never do something like that, no matter how frustrated she was with Lady Pendleton. The chief and I have been best friends over the years. He has never let my family down, especially after my wife's death. He's been like a second father to Jenny."

"Don't worry, Mac. I know Jenny's friends will back her up. We'll get to the bottom of this."

Brenda was determined that this case would not tear apart Sweetfern Harbor and especially not Detective Rivers' life. Jenny's father had been a widower so young and had known enough tragedy for one lifetime. They promised to keep in touch in case any new information surfaced that he needed help with.

A few days later, Brenda answered the phone to Mac's joyful greeting. "They cleared her. They are not going to file any charges against Jenny." His voice filled with relief. "Bob Ingram just gave me the good news and I had to let you know. You were right, Molly and Hope insisted she was just blowing off steam. The chief questioned Edward Graham and he agreed Jenny was frustrated and just had to take it out on someone. He happened to be the one she chose since he was Lady Pendleton's lawyer. No one found anything substantive against Jenny."

After ending the call with Mac, she dialed Edward Graham and asked if he had time to see her for a few minutes. His voice had an unusual lilt to it and he agreed to see her in half an hour. When Brenda opened the door to the waiting room at Edward's office, she heard laughter coming from his office. She recognized the voice of his receptionist.

"I have to tell you, Tracy, I never expected to live long enough to see Lady Pendleton dead. It all looked too easy." Tracy agreed and then went out into the waiting room where she saw Brenda getting ready to sit down.

"I'm sure Edward will see you now," she said.

Brenda wondered what happened to Mr. Graham. She had never heard Tracy refer to him by his first name. It seemed that everyone had become more relaxed in the days since

Lady Pendleton's death. Surely there is one person who is sorry to see her go, she thought. No one came to mind. She went into Edward's office. He greeted her with a wide smile.

"Come on in, Brenda, I'm just wrapping up the many lawsuits Lady Pendleton filed against everyone."

"I guess William will take them over?" she asked.

The hearty laughter startled her. "William has no intentions of pressing charges against anyone in Sweetfern Harbor. I'll meet with the judge and William, and go from there. I don't see anyone going to court over any of it."

Brenda went into her sleuth mode. "Did you tell Detective Rivers you were supposed to meet with Lady Pendleton the morning of her death?"

His face grew serious. He moved to clasp his hands on the desk. "Yes, I had to be in court and couldn't meet with her. She understood I couldn't always keep appointments with her since there are times court calls. It didn't happen often. She could tolerate only so much of anyone not obeying her at the snap of her fingers." He displayed a lopsided grin and then grew serious again. "Why do you ask?"

"Mac asked me to assist in a minor way with the case. I had a little experience back in Michigan." Edward had already heard the bed and breakfast owner had been an assistant to a private investigator. He shifted in the chair and repeated his story about being in court. "I looked at the court docket for that day," said Brenda. "The case you were in court for was the first one that came up and within a few minutes it was dismissed. Where did you go after you left the courthouse?"

"I came back here to my office. Lady Pendleton and I had already rescheduled so I didn't bother to tell her I had more free time than expected. I didn't see her at all that day."

"Did you see other clients when you returned? And I suppose Tracy was here to verify you came back here."

Edward's face hardened slightly, realizing that Brenda was questioning his story. "Actually, Tracy had to take her mother for tests at the hospital. She was not here that day." He pulled out a notepad and wrote down three names. "These are the clients I saw that morning. One had not gotten the message I wouldn't be in and caught me by chance. I called the other two to let them know I had time to see them that morning."

Brenda smiled. "I'll give these names to Mac. I hope you understand that everyone around town is being grilled by me or by Mac." She stood and shook his hand. His cheerful demeanor returned.

"I do understand. I suppose it's still a shock to know she is dead and we're all trying to find our way in a new normal."

On the way back to Sheffield Bed and Breakfast, Brenda thought about Edward Graham. She was sure Mac would dismiss him as a suspect once she reported her findings. Besides, the lawyer depended on Lady Pendleton's fees which said he wouldn't want her dead, and it was clear he wouldn't lose any business since William Pendleton had retained him to work on the property deeds.

Driving down Main Street, Brenda tried to recapture the feelings she had the first day she came into town. This time she parked in front of Morning Sun Coffee and went inside. A few customers sat chatting at the tables and in the armchairs with their beverages. Logan delivered a plate of finger sandwiches to a couple with two children. He waved at Brenda.

"Do you want your usual, Brenda?"

"Today, I want a double latté. And ask Molly if she has any blueberry bread left, please." A couple of minutes later, he set the steaming cup in front of her. "When do you get a break?" she asked Logan.

He raised an eyebrow, clearly curious, and glanced at the clock on the wall. "In about five minutes I'll finish up. I'll join you then if you want." He was still busy and left her to finish her latté in peace.

Brenda savored her hot beverage and felt the caffeine begin to perk her up. Molly came over to greet her and sat down. She set a small plate of blueberry bread in front of Brenda, who eagerly took a bite of the delicious summer specialty.

She knew she only had a few minutes with Molly before Logan returned, so she got down to business. "Molly, were you here at the shop the day Lady Pendleton died?"

"I was. I ran up to take a look but by the time I got there, the crowd was too big already. So I headed back here and waited for news the rest of that morning. Later I did run to the post office and on my way back stopped to chat briefly with Jenny at Blossoms and said hi to Hope at her shop. By then they weren't letting anyone near the crime scene anymore."

"What about the day before? Isn't Thursday the day the Pendletons usually came in?"

Molly leaned back and thought for a few seconds. "Actually, I was in and out most of that afternoon. I left instructions with Logan to make sure Lady Pendleton got her package of coffee. We have to import it special and then roast it to get the right flavor. She always wanted it perfectly sealed up. She was particular that way."

Brenda was curious to learn that Logan had manned the shop solo while Molly was gone. "She probably had the usual while she was here. Same thing every time," she said. "It was always a cappuccino. William was more adventurous and he liked an iced caramel mocha, or something sweet like that. They never stayed very long, but I'm sure Logan could tell you whether that was true that day."

Brenda was satisfied and wrote down a few quick notes.

"Do you think something happened while she was here? Does Mac know who did it?" asked Molly eagerly.

"A lot has to happen before anyone is charged with murder," Brenda laughed fondly. "Why? Do you have any ideas about who did it?"

Molly looked taken aback for a moment, then chuckled. "I'm surprised you are asking me that question. If you want to know how to make a great cup of coffee, ask me anytime. But all I know about this thing is what I hear from the rumors flying around."

"Well," replied Brenda, "you let me know if those rumors pop up with anything good." Molly offered her another latté, but Brenda saw Logan folding his apron and declined Molly's offer. Molly went back to the counter as Logan sat down at Brenda's table, an iced drink in his hand.

"Molly tells me you were in charge when Lady Pendleton and William came in the day before she died," said Brenda. "Did anyone else come in during that time?"

Logan took a long pull of his drink through the straw, gazing out the window while he thought. She noticed he did not meet her eyes as he said, "Several customers came and went that afternoon but when the Pendletons came in, no one else was in here. I served them their usual drinks. Always a cappuccino for Lady Pendleton and usually something like an iced mocha for William. They had their drinks, took the special coffee bean order, and left."

Brenda knew she had to ask a delicate question that she hadn't been ready to ask of Molly. "Do you keep any poison in the storeroom, like for pest control?"

Logan's youthful face turned ashen as he looked straight at her. "We have a pest control service that comes after hours every month. I think they spray something in the store room, like at the corners of the room and near the drains." He clasped his hands and then unclasped them and sipped his drink. "In answer to your question, there is no poison kept here at all."

He was back to avoiding her gaze again, and there was something strange about the way he had phrased his reply. No poison was stored at the coffee shop, certainly, but that didn't seem to mean there was no poison on the premises.

"I'm not saying the poison came from here. In an investigation, questions have to be asked. Sometimes they can send the wrong message. I hope you understand."

Logan's face relaxed. "I thought maybe you were thinking I poisoned Lady Pendleton's drink."

Brenda let the comment pass. If anyone had done that, it would have been Logan. "I'm not accusing you of anything. Detective Rivers and I are trying to find any place that may be a source of poison. If none is kept here, then we can move on." She smiled reassuringly and Logan grinned back, relieved.

Just as she drove up the driveway to the bed and breakfast, her cell phone rang.

"I'm glad I caught you, Brenda. The coroner is positive it was antifreeze in Lady Pendleton's system. It's bad enough that everyone in town had a motive to want her dead but when it comes to antifreeze, it will be like trying to find a needle in a haystack. It's not an uncommon substance here since winters can be harsh."

Brenda read frustration in his voice. "Don't give up yet. There will be something neither of us expects that will lead right to the person or persons responsible."

"You're right, Brenda, though I don't give up easily. I know that the footwork can be tedious. I'm about to close down for the day." Brenda felt hesitation in his voice. "If you're not too busy later this evening, I know a great place to grab a bite to eat."

Brenda's heart skipped a beat. "That sounds like a good idea. We could both use a break."

Mac felt a surge of life course through him. Now all he had to do was explain to his best friend Police Chief Bob Ingram why, for the first time in years, he had to miss their weekly pool playing night.

chapter six

After dinner out with Mac Rivers, Brenda arrived home around midnight. She heard a shuffling sound coming from the Gathering Room and wondered which guest was wandering around at this time of night. Perhaps it was Phyllis or Carrie waiting to hear about what they termed her "first date."

Suddenly, she caught sight of a figure moving quickly. Her heart picked up a beat and rather than call out, she kept perfectly still and waited in the darkened foyer.

She heard the shuffling of papers or something similar in the office. She became alarmed when she heard the click of the drawer in the corner desk that she used. She knew from the sound that it was the one drawer she always kept locked. Her notepad with the suspect list and a few other notes about anyone who might be involved in the murder was in that drawer.

She peered around the corner. So far, the intruder did not realize she was there. "Who's there?" she called from the doorway.

As if struck by a bolt of lightning, the figure raced for the opposite door that led through a sunroom and to the outside. In a split second, she was staring at the swinging door the intruder had just brushed through. She followed, yelling "Stop!" She heard her own voice echo in the moonlight and she saw nothing. Turning back inside, she dialed the detective.

When Mac arrived a few minutes later, he bounded up the steps to the Sheffield and she was grateful to see him at the door.

"Hi, again," she said lamely.

"I wish it were under different circumstances," Mac said with a grimace as he moved toward the office. She followed, her heart still pounding, and watched as he snapped pictures of the disarray around the area of the corner desk.

"I keep that drawer locked at all times. As far as I know, I am the only one with a key," said Brenda.

Mac turned to her and then gestured toward the split drawer. "Whoever it was didn't need a key. It looks like you'll need to repair it later." He asked why she kept that one drawer locked and Brenda explained her reasons.

"I keep my notes here where it is handy if I decide I need to talk to someone else. It saves me steps going back upstairs. Carrie and Phyllis have seen me put things in here and lock it. They've never asked questions or shown any real interest as far as I can recall."

After discussing her poor description of the person searching through the desk, Mac made sure the sunroom door was secured. "Can we lock this office until morning? I want a team to go over everything with a fine-toothed comb. We can only hope the intruder didn't wear gloves."

"It was hard to tell in the dark. I wish I had flipped on the light just before I called out."

"That may have put you in more danger than you bargained for."

His eyes lingered on her face for a few seconds, his brow wrinkled in concern. He noted animation in her tinted cheeks and her amber eyes sparkled. She made a good investigator, he thought. He was surprised by the strength of his certainty about having her on this case, and wondered if his personal feelings were betrayed too much.

Brenda looked at him curiously. "Is there more?" she asked.

"No, I believe that everything is secure." He checked the locked office door to make sure it was tightly closed, then turned to look at her. "Brenda, I don't like the idea of you here when you've just scared an intruder. Let me stay here, I'll guard the door."

She searched his face in consternation and said, "What would my guests say in the morning when they saw an armed detective blocking the entrance? No, Mac. I'll be fine."

He stood at the front door and worriedly looked out into the darkened streets of Sweetfern Harbor. "You may be right, but I won't take any chances. I'll be out there in my car until morning in case they try to return."

That night as Brenda tried to relax in bed, she kept seeing the shadowed figure in her mind. Lithe, slender, somewhat tall, and above all, quick on his feet. It could match any number of people in town. She planned to start with Hope Williams, whom she had arranged to meet with the next day.

Sleepily, she also thought of another figure in the dark. Not the intruder's slim build, but the broad shoulders and curling blond hair of Detective Mac Rivers outside in his car, guarding the Sheffield Bed and Breakfast. With a smile, she drifted off to sleep.

Brenda came downstairs earlier than usual the next morning. She knew there would be a slew of questions. She was right.

"Why is the office locked up? What is this all about?" asked Phyllis. She pointed to Mac's car, still parked at the curb. Carrie peeped over Brenda's shoulder. As they looked outside, Mac raised one slightly weary hand and waved.

Brenda didn't mince words. "We had an intruder last night. I called Mac and he came right over."

"I thought you were out with Mac," said Phyllis.

"Well, that was earlier in the night. I surprised the intruder when I got home..."

"How did the date go?" Brenda's night out was somehow far more interesting than the fact that someone had broken into the Sheffield Bed and Breakfast the night before.

"We can talk about it later. Right now, we must redirect the guests, Mac's team will be coming to examine the scene soon. Phyllis, perhaps after breakfast you can explain the situation and invite everyone out for coffee and tea in the back garden. We need everyone to steer clear of the front hall and office." She turned to Carrie. "If anyone is not in the mood for tea in the garden, perhaps you can suggest sights around town they may be interested in."

Carrie agreed readily. "There is a small handicrafts festival just off Main Street today. There will be plenty of handcrafted things to buy as well as food vendors."

As Phyllis busied herself making a short list of supplies she would need to set out in the rose garden for tea and coffee, it dawned on the housekeeper that she should be asking Brenda about more than her night out with Mac Rivers. She wanted to ask what the intruder could have been looking for, but Brenda's demeanor told her she wouldn't get her answers.

By early afternoon, Mac and his team had completed their work and the front hall and sitting room were opened once more to the guests. The detective had also discreetly phoned a woodworking friend in town who would repair the drawer.

After a thorough search and interviewing everyone who used the office, it was clear that Brenda's notes were the only thing missing.

Outside, she told Mac she was still planning to see Hope Williams. "I don't think either of us has really interrogated her yet," she pointed out. He agreed and gave her a ride to Main Street.

When she entered Sweet Treats Bakery, Hope was behind the counter arranging freshly baked cupcakes. Brenda never tired of the sweet aroma of buttercream frosting that filled the shop. Hope greeted her with a smile.

"When you have a moment, I'd like to speak with you. Mac has asked me to help with the questioning. Do you mind?"

"Of course not," said Hope. "I wondered when my turn was coming." She wiped her hands on her apron and called to a young girl who emerged from the back. "Tina, will you mind the front counter for a few minutes?"

Tina came up to help the few customers browsing the baked goods, and Hope and Brenda settled in at a small table in the back corner of the shop.

"Did you speak with Lady Pendleton any time shortly before her death?" asked Brenda.

"She liked to personally give notice when she was about to raise the rent, or to let you know if she had some kind of complaint. I heard she had been to see a few other shop owners already, so I knew she was coming. I actually wanted to see her this time around, because I planned to point out the unfairness of the lawsuit she filed against Jenny." Hope's bitter laugh reminded Brenda of how much unfinished business had been on the table at the time of the woman's death.

"And did you get a chance to tell her all that?"

"I tried. Later, when she came in, I tried to give her a piece of my mind. I was sure she was going to raise my rent double, in retaliation. Then she really surprised me. She asked if I wanted to meet her for lunch the next day. I have no idea what motivated her to ask me that."

How strange, Brenda mused. Perhaps there was something more to Lady Pendleton than first appeared. "Did you meet the next day?"

Hope nodded her head. "We met for lunch. I brought her a cupcake as a peace offering."

When Brenda asked what they discussed during lunch, Hope told her they had said very little and her conclusion was that Lady Pendleton's motive was to show everyone she favored Hope over other shop owners. Hope threw up her hands in frustration. "I have no idea why she did that right after I accosted her like that. I have to say, she did pay for the meal which surprised me."

"Interesting. By the way, where were you last night?" Brenda asked casually, hoping to catch Hope off guard.

"I was sound asleep in bed," she said, taken aback.

"Can anyone verify that?" It had not escaped her notice that Hope was slim and agile, similar to the physique of the intruder. She had also noticed those qualities in the way she moved about while taking care of customers in the bakery.

Hope's face turned pink. "I'm not married. I have no children. I live alone. No one can verify that I was sound asleep in my bed all night."

Brenda's cell phone rang. She excused herself, stood up, and took the call a few steps away from Hope. When she realized who it was, she went back and thanked Hope for the chat. "Mac may want to speak to you as well," she told her.

She headed for the door. "Mac, I can talk now," said Brenda.

"It has been determined that Lady Pendleton was not poisoned over a period of time. It was definitely a massive, one-time dosage, according to the coroner."

"That does narrow things down. What do you think about

Hope Williams? I just interviewed her. She gave Lady Pendleton a freshly baked cupcake the day before her death. She could easily have laced the frosting with antifreeze. She had a motive when rents went up."

"Every shop owner had a motive. It had to be someone who saw her a few hours before her death and who used it against her. We have Pete, William, Hope, and a few others who interacted with her in the twenty-four hours prior to her death."

"What about Pete Graham? He certainly knows the grudges everyone in town held against Lady Pendleton," said Brenda. "He was the go-between for Phyllis and William. Most importantly of all, we know that is the one thing he kept quiet about. Maybe he was bribed to do something to her by one of them. Maybe they knew something about Pete."

Mac was silent for a few seconds. "An interesting theory. But he didn't give her food or drink before she died." Mac made for a good devil's advocate, thought Brenda, relishing the quick back and forth of their talk and the easy way they seemed to work together. However, the suspect list was beginning to entwine into a tight knot.

Brenda changed the subject, knowing she would have a long talk with Pete Graham later. "Any leads on my intruder from last night?"

"There were no fingerprints at all. Not even a shoe print."

Brenda felt dejected. "I've been wondering about the people who live around here. Carrie knew I locked that drawer but she isn't tall enough to match the figure I saw."

"Molly Lindsey is slim and moves easily. Maybe she broke into your place. Let's meet as soon as possible—there's been a development. I believe that when we solve Lady Pendleton's murder, we will have the answers about your intruder, too."

They agreed to meet at the station in fifteen minutes. When Brenda got there she found Mac with his elbows on the desk, flipping through his notes from the past few days.

Brenda had not commented when he brought up Molly's name and was curious to know why he thought she was edging to the top of his list.

"I've asked Molly Lindsey to come down here for another interview. In the meantime, I want to fill you in. We found a paper cup from Morning Sun Coffee in the Pendleton home. It was in the trash can of Lady Pendleton's office in the south wing. I sent the cup to the lab for testing."

"I'm interested to hear Molly's side of it all," said Brenda, dismayed. "I find it hard to believe she is a murderer."

Moments later, a knock on the door of his office told them that Molly Lindsey had arrived. She glanced at Brenda when Mac told her to sit down. "Do you want anything to drink?" he asked. She shook her head no.

"We'll get right to it. How much did you know about the lawsuit that Lady Pendleton had filed against Jenny?" he asked.

"I knew every detail. At least, I knew as much as Jenny did. She told me and Hope Williams everything. We're best friends, after all. You know that." Brenda watched Molly's response closely.

"You told me that Logan Tucker was in charge the day Lady Pendleton came in to pick up her weekly coffee order," said Brenda. Molly nodded yes. "Were you in and out, or were you away from the shop all afternoon? I know I've asked these questions, but for Mac's sake, will you tell me again?"

"I came back in a couple of times. I met with Jenny at Blossoms and stayed a half hour or so after a quick trip to the post office. Then I went to Hope's bakery. We spoke a few minutes. Mostly about the lawsuit, but that wasn't unusual."

"We found a cup at the Pendleton home that Lady Pendleton drank her coffee from that day," said Mac.

Molly looked up quickly. "That would have been Logan—

he was in the shop when Lady Pendleton and William came in."

Molly clenched her fingers and then opened her hands wide as if stretching them. Brenda watched her clasp them again and again in the few seconds before anyone spoke.

"Someone in this town poisoned Lady Pendleton," said the detective.

"Maybe she poisoned herself," suggested Molly, not quite meeting anyone's eyes. "Everyone knows how miserable a person she was. I can just see her ending her own life."

Mac leaned forward. "I'll keep that in mind, Molly. But in the meantime, don't leave town. I'll have more questions for you." Molly's face paled. She stood and walked slowly from the office.

When the door closed, Mac said, "I believe it was Molly. Maybe Logan served the coffee, but she could have been the one who prepared it. Or maybe she laced the coffee beans that Lady Pendleton picked up that afternoon. Interestingly enough, we haven't found those coffee beans anywhere, so we can't test them. And Molly showed extreme nervousness, as if she has something to hide." He leaned back in his chair. "I'm going to prepare a warrant for her arrest."

Brenda stared at him. "If she drank laced coffee, why didn't William ingest the poison as well? Besides, what evidence do you have to arrest Molly?"

"I don't have enough—not yet. I'm simply going to prepare a warrant. Once the cup gets back from the lab I believe I'll have the evidence against her and will then serve the warrant."

"You seem pretty confident, Mac. I think there are more suspects to question again to be sure."

"I'll consider that, Brenda, but I feel sure Molly is the one involved."

On her way home, Brenda thought about the handsome man who was beginning to steal her heart and the confusion of this sudden development in the case. She pulled over to the curb, trying to think. The detective was intent on arresting someone who may have the means and motive for murder, but it wasn't a slam dunk by any means. Could he be trying to divert everyone's attention from his daughter, Jenny?

She had not asked Mac on what grounds his supervisor had cleared Jenny from suspicion. His daughter was good friends with the bakery owner as well as the owner of the coffee shop. Could she have worked with her friends to poison Lady Pendleton, or tried to frame one of her friends for the murder?

Brenda thought through her suspicions of Jenny, but in the end, none of them were truly viable. She knew it wouldn't have been the norm to serve refreshments in the florist's shop and so far, no one had mentioned Jenny sneaking around with antifreeze.

The biggest puzzle was why Mac was so sure Molly Lindsey was the one who poisoned Lady Pendleton when Logan had served the coffee drinks that day. But she didn't have time to answer that question, because it was time to visit Pete Graham. Brenda glanced at her watch. She knew he went into work very early in the morning and was home shortly after noon. She dialed his number.

"I'm running a few errands but will be finished in about twenty minutes," he said. "I can come over to the bed and breakfast if you'd like."

"I'm on my way back there now. Come around to the rose garden and we can talk there."

Brenda asked the kitchen for a pitcher of lemonade and a small plate of cookies. She headed to the garden with the tray to wait for Pete Graham. Perhaps it would be different to talk with him away from the usual crowds who waited for the latest gossip around town.

She looked up when she heard his voice and invited Pete to sit down with her at the small wrought iron table under the arbor of climbing roses in shades of crimson and pale pink. She poured lemonade into a glass and handed it to him.

He took a long drink, savoring its coolness in the heat of the summer day. "This lemonade is the best in town. Someday I'd like to have your chef tell me what her secret ingredient is," he said.

"She may not want to tell you, in case you tell everyone," said Brenda in a joking tone. She grew serious. "As you know, I've been helping Mac with the investigation. I want to ask you some questions about the letters you carried between William and Phyllis."

"Sure," he said. He sipped the cold drink and waited.

"When did the exchanges begin?"

"I've been doing that for William and Phyllis for over two years. I was careful and until that final day, Lady Pendleton had no idea our game was going on."

"It seems that is the one secret you kept quite well, if it went on for over two years."

"I thought William needed a little fun in his life. I can't imagine what it must have been like to be married to someone like Lady Pendleton. Besides, he offered me a reward." When Brenda asked about the reward, he told her that several times a year William paid him a modest sum of money for keeping their secret. "He said he couldn't afford much, but he said that when his wife died, he would inherit most of her wealth. He promised I wouldn't have long to wait. At that point, I could expect more of a reward than I could imagine." Pete's grin covered his face. "He told me just the other day how much he appreciated my discretion on his behalf. In less than a month I will get my real reward." He chuckled. "I surprised myself how well I kept that secret, but money talks, as they say."

Brenda immediately wondered why William Pendleton had not revealed this part of the arrangement to Detective Rivers, and resolved to figure out how it fit into the puzzle.

Moreover, Pete seemed unaware of how odd it sounded that William had seemed so sure Lady Pendleton would die first, and soon.

But in the meantime, as they kept talking, she realized Pete had nothing more to add other than the usual town gossip. After another glass of lemonade, they said goodbye and he walked back toward town. Brenda sat under the sweet-scented rose arbor, watching the ocean and thinking back to the cocktail party after the boat race, back before life in Sweetfern Harbor had become so complicated.

chapter seven

The next morning, Brenda drove to the Pendleton mansion, wanting to solve an important question she had been left with after her talk with Pete. Had William Pendleton been hinting to Pete Graham that he knew his wife would die soon?

The grand house was quiet and she relished the chance to observe its luxurious surroundings. She could only imagine what was on the inside of the place. When she knocked, however, she was informed that William was not at home, and so she took her time climbing back into her car, taking in the elaborately landscaped gardens and elegant views.

William Pendleton was a wealthy man indeed if Lady Pendleton had left this all to him. Not to mention he now owned most of Sweetfern Harbor as well.

On her way home, Brenda did a double take when she noticed Carrie's cousin Kelly from New York chatting with Logan Tucker on the sidewalk. It struck her as odd that he should be out socializing a block away from the coffee shop when she knew that Molly was not at Morning Sun at the moment. Molly had been delivering pastries to the Sheffield Bed and Breakfast and stopping in for one of her chats with her mother and Carrie. She had to have still been at the bed and breakfast since Brenda hadn't been gone long.

Kelly Martin threw her head back and laughed at something Logan said. He gave her his trademark roguish grin and turned back in the direction of the coffee shop. Brenda slowed down and gave Kelly time to walk a half block ahead before she pulled over and offered her a ride back to Sheffield Bed and Breakfast. Brenda opted to refrain from mentioning seeing the two together.

"How long are you planning to stay in Sweetfern Harbor?" Brenda asked as they drove.

"I'm trying to convince Carrie to come back with me to New York. We could share an apartment and she could break out of her rut. If I can't get her to commit to it soon, it probably won't happen. I have to leave in a day or so."

"She seems very happy here," said Brenda.

"She likes her job, and you too, Brenda, but she once had big dreams. When her parents died suddenly several years ago she lost all ambition. She always dreamed of becoming a pharmacist. Her parents had saved money for her education and her father encouraged her to follow her dreams. He was a pharmacist and I guess he saw her potential."

"I had no idea," said Brenda. "I agree she should try and reach her goals. Is she interested in going back with you?"

"I think so. She just needs a push," said Kelly.

Brenda pulled into her parking space behind the bed and breakfast. Kelly thanked her for the ride and for her hospitality during her stay. Brenda sat in her car thinking about everything she learned from Kelly Martin. When she entered the back door, she heard raised voices coming from down the hallway. The chef glanced up as Brenda hurried to find out what the disturbance was all about.

In the sitting room, she found Phyllis facing Mac Rivers. Phyllis had never looked so distressed.

"I can't believe you think my own daughter is a murderer,

Mac Rivers," said Phyllis. "You're saying that just to excuse your own daughter. Jenny was the one who was in the biggest fight against Lady Pendleton."

Brenda stepped forward bravely, determined to speak the truth no matter what it cost her. "You know she's right, Mac. Jenny was the one complaining most about her. She even voiced threats to several people that she would take care of Lady Pendleton." She only hoped that Mac understood that she had not revealed any of his suspicions to Phyllis. Perhaps he had come by to give her the news in person, out of respect.

Mac's face hardened. "I am not taking anyone's side. If the evidence points to Morning Sun, then I will move forward even if I have to arrest your daughter, Phyllis." He turned and stalked out of the room. They listened in silence until the door slammed behind him.

Carrie stepped toward Phyllis and put her arm around her shaking shoulders. "I'm sorry, Brenda," Phyllis said, trying to wipe away her tears, "but the detective is completely wrong about Molly. Logan loves working for her and has never spoken an ill word against her. She just doesn't have it in her to commit murder."

Brenda nodded in mute sympathy. She didn't know what to think and her heart hurt to think of her loyalties being torn between her staff and the man who was starting to steal her heart. "Did Molly leave or is she still here?" Brenda asked.

Carrie told her she had left just before Mac came in to give Phyllis the news. Phyllis broke into tears again and Brenda encouraged Carrie to take her into the back office and give her some hot tea. "I'll check back soon. In the meantime, Phyllis, please don't worry. I think Mac is wrong about his suspicions of Molly. It will all get straightened out soon."

The next morning, Brenda walked to Morning Sun Coffee. She wanted a private talk with Molly to reassure her. Brenda was certain Mac was willfully ignoring anyone else who had motive and means to do the act. When she went inside, she saw Logan behind the counter. She waited until several customers made their orders. She hung back until they had picked up their coffees and left the shop. He then asked her for her order.

"I'm looking for Molly. Is she here?"

"She's not here right now."

In a low voice, Brenda said, "Logan, do you think you can be straight with me? How do you feel about working for Molly?"

He assured her that Molly was a great boss. "Even when I come in late, she never complains unless the town has a big gala going on or something."

"Are you and Carrie close?"

Logan's grin spread across his face. "We're in love. I know it sounds corny but we have dated since freshman year in high school. I stood by her when her parents died. Carrie had a terrible time of it for a while."

Brenda encouraged him to give her details. He told her that Carrie stayed in her parents' home at first, since it was where she had grown up. The house's mortgage was owned by Lady Pendleton, not surprisingly. Apparently, when Carrie had a hard time continuing mortgage payments, the whole town chipped in to help her out.

"She even used the college education money her parents had saved for her. Eventually, it all became too much for her and of course, Lady Pendleton stepped right in. She headed for the bank and foreclosed on the property. Carrie was forced from her own home, if you can believe it. First her parents, then no hopes of college and no home, too."

For confirmation of Kelly's story, Brenda asked Logan what field of study Carrie had planned to pursue.

"She wanted to be a pharmacist like her dad. She is the smartest person I know and she aced every subject she studied. Lady Pendleton took it all away from her." His voice took on a dark, bitter tone Brenda had heard before. For perhaps the first time, his trademark grin had vanished.

"Do you think Carrie was ready for that kind of science work? What was her favorite subject in high school?"

It was then Logan laughed. "She was more than ready to be a pharmacist because she just loved chemistry. I think she liked outsmarting the guys that made fun of her during lab times. She showed me a couple of things about chemistry I never knew before. I wouldn't have passed without her help."

"I don't doubt Carrie is a smart girl. Thanks for filling me in on her past. I'm so sorry she lost her parents, and her home. Do me a favor, tell Molly to give me a call when she gets a minute." She left Morning Sun, Logan tending the counter on his own and still looking sad about his girlfriend's tragic past.

When Brenda returned to the bed and breakfast, she went into the sitting room, where afternoon tea was being served. It was one of her favorite treats and something that brought guests back many times. Several guests sipped hot tea from dainty teacups by the front windows, talking in small clusters, and Phyllis set a tray of mini sandwiches on the table. Brenda waited until she left the room and then followed her down the hallway. She called to her housekeeper who turned and smiled. Brenda was glad to see her puffy red eyes had recovered.

"I just want you to know that I really think Mac is barking up the wrong tree, Phyllis. We'll get this all straightened out soon. Molly is not someone who could kill." When her housekeeper shuddered in distress, Brenda reached for her arm and squeezed it. "I promise you the real killer will be found out and it won't be your daughter."

Once back in her apartment, Brenda thought about the missing list of her suspects. She had written down comments next to names that were her early thoughts. She breathed a sigh of relief to remember she hadn't written any important reasons for suspecting any of them. She had mainly noted personalities and where they each worked. She sat down in her easy chair to think things out. She quickly dismissed Molly Lindsey, Jenny Rivers, and Hope Williams.

Carrie Martin loomed ahead of everyone since Brenda now knew her background. Despite her thwarted college plans, perhaps Carrie knew more about dangerous chemicals than people suspected. She would have known about the coffee that Lady Pendleton liked since Molly mentioned that among her friends. Maybe she was in the coffee shop with her boyfriend Logan when he served Lady Pendleton her hot cup of coffee that day. Were they both in it together? It had to be airtight: opportunity, motive, and means. She dialed Mac Rivers.

"I have some new information, Mac," said Brenda. "If you have time, I'd like to come by."

When she walked into his office, Mac was relieved to realize Brenda Sheffield didn't hold ill will toward him. After he had departed the bed and breakfast in a cold fury, he had been chagrined to think how he might have jeopardized their relationship somehow.

Brenda exchanged a smile with the detective and sat down. "I apologize for the way I confronted you at the bed and breakfast. I know you are just doing your job."

"I want to apologize in return. I guess when it comes to one's daughter, a father is her greatest defender. I know Jenny had nothing to do with the death of Lady Pendleton but I also know how it looked to you and Phyllis."

"I'm glad we're back on track. I need to tell you what I've learned about Carrie Martin."

Brenda was not ready to tell him of her interview with Pete Graham. She wanted to talk to William first about the matter of the inheritance. She told him of her conversations with Kelly Martin and Logan Tucker, which led her to Carrie Martin.

"I am positive Carrie did not break into my desk but she could have suspected my notes had something to do with the murder. She could have told Logan or even Kelly where to get my notes in case there was anything against any of them." Brenda continued as Mac listened, deep in thought. "Maybe Carrie was in the shop with Logan when he served coffee to Lady Pendleton. He told me that Carrie was a whiz in chemistry class and she helped him pass the course."

Mac leaned forward. "You have some good points here." His forehead furrowed and he looked directly at Brenda. "But there's something else. Lab reports came back a few minutes ago. The antifreeze was in the coffee she got from Morning Sun. There were traces of it found in the coffee cup in Lady Pendleton's wastebasket. Now I'm interested in a chat with Carrie. She could have been with Logan that day, though he didn't mention her. Is she working this afternoon?"

"She should be in her office. She usually answers reservation emails about this time."

Brenda followed Mac's police car back to the bed and breakfast. When they entered, no one was in the foyer or the office. Brenda peeked into the sitting room. One guest was curled up in the love seat reading a book. She didn't look up when Brenda glanced in.

"Wait here, Mac, and I'll go down to the kitchen and ask if anyone has seen Carrie."

The chef was chopping vegetables. She smiled at Brenda which told her that she approved of the way her boss had stood up for Molly. She told Brenda she had not seen Carrie since lunch. Brenda then went down the narrow hallway and knocked on the door to Phyllis's.

"I haven't seen Carrie this afternoon. She takes her break early to mid-afternoon. Maybe she walked downtown," said Phyllis, who was polishing a teapot. "I'm waiting for William. He's picking me up and we're going to the museum this afternoon."

Brenda smiled at her. Phyllis relaxed more now that her relationship with William Pendleton was out in the open. Gossip about the relationship and approval for the two's love was almost as common in Sweetfern Harbor as gossip about murder suspects. Brenda returned to Mac, frustrated.

"Let's go check at the coffee shop. Sometimes she visits Logan there when she has time."

"Get in with me and I'll bring you back when we find her," said Mac.

When they got to Morning Sun Coffee, Molly looked a little wary of them as she asked them for their orders.

"We're looking for Carrie and I thought maybe she was down here hanging out with Logan on her break," said Brenda. She looked around and didn't see Logan. "Is Logan off this afternoon?"

"He's probably with Carrie. Her cousin Kelly is leaving in a little while to go back home to New York. Logan and Carrie mentioned giving her a send-off down at the bus station." She gave an apologetic grin. "I'm sorry. I didn't even ask them what time Kelly was supposed to be leaving." She looked at the detective. Her face turned serious. "I'm on pins and needles wondering if and when you are going to arrest me. It's worse waiting than knowing."

Detective Rivers jerked slightly at her question. "It won't be any time soon, Molly. I'm still investigating everyone."

"That's good to know. I worried about the shop and who would keep it going. Logan can never seem to come in on time and he has no clue of how to keep inventory at the right level." She smiled. "At least with William in charge of the lease we can all relax and stop worrying about unexpected rent increases and build our businesses the way we want."

With that, Brenda and Mac quickly left for the bus depot.

chapter eight

They drove through the streets until reaching the edge of town where the bus depot was located. Two buses were parked. People were getting onto one of them. The bus was ready to pull out. Mac parked and they hurried toward the bus. Searching the faces of those boarding, neither saw Kelly.

"Let's go inside. Maybe she is getting her ticket. The bus for New York is not filled yet," said Brenda. She pointed to the second bus. Mac hurried over to it and stepped inside. She saw him flash his badge and he scanned the faces of the passengers on board, then he stepped back down.

Inside the depot, they spotted Logan at the ticket counter. Carrie stood to his side. Kelly sat on the bench intent on her iPad. Mac stood on the other side of Logan and asked him if he was buying a ticket for Kelly. Brenda talked with Kelly who told her she was waiting for Carrie and Logan to get their tickets.

"We're all leaving for New York. Both of them decided to come with me." Her face lit up with excitement. "I'm so glad Carrie decided to finally follow her dreams. Logan was determined to come with her. He doesn't want any big city guy getting his girl. At least, that's what he said."

Brenda rushed to Mac and whispered the news. Mac moved to Carrie's side. Brenda hurried to stand by Logan. The young couple looked surprised to see them.

"You aren't going anywhere, Carrie. I'm putting you under arrest for the murder of Priscilla Pendleton." He took his handcuffs out and pulled her wrists together behind her back, fastening them securely.

"What?" Logan yelled. "She's no murderer. Let her go! She's on her way to New York to finally follow her dream. There is no way Carrie killed that old lady."

Kelly rushed to her cousin's side. "What's going on?" she asked in alarm.

"Carrie is being arrested for the murder of Lady Pendleton," Brenda replied. Kelly's eyes opened wide matching her gaping mouth.

"Carrie is not the murderer. You have the wrong person." Logan's voice rose to an anguished shout and he began to draw a crowd.

Security was called while Mac radioed for a backup squad car. Carrie's eyes filled with tears but with handcuffs on her she had no way of wiping them from her cheeks. Kelly quickly hugged her and carefully reached to dry her cousin's tears.

"I can't stay. The bus is leaving soon, Carrie. My job is waiting back in New York. My boss told me if I don't come home soon I won't have a job. I have to go but I will check with Logan to find out what happens with you. I know you didn't do it." She hugged Carrie again and tears flowed between the cousins. Two cops entered and one immediately escorted Carrie to the car. The other one snapped handcuffs onto Logan at Mac's orders, arresting him for disorderly conduct.

"Good," he yelled at Mac as he was walked slowly to the exit. "If she goes to jail, I'm not leaving her there. She's innocent and you have no proof she killed anyone."

The crowd was held spellbound with these events, but the bus station security and the cops moved everyone back.

Brenda noticed Kelly. She appeared helpless as well as confused as to what she should do. Brenda stepped over to her.

"I understand how you feel, Kelly. You have a job to go home to and you aren't that far from Sweetfern Harbor. Call me for any updates if you want to." She passed her a business card with the number of Sheffield Bed and Breakfast printed on it. Kelly smiled and thanked her, trying to hide her anguish. She hurried to the bus without looking back.

Logan called back to her. "Don't worry, Kelly, they have the wrong person and Mac Rivers will soon know that. He's made a big mistake."

Brenda got into Mac's car, still a little shell-shocked from the shouting confrontation. "I have to tell you something, Mac. I was hoping to confirm this first with William Pendleton, but everything is moving so fast now..." She told him of her conversation with Pete Graham. "I'm not saying you don't have your reasons for arresting Carrie, but I really think there could be something between William and Pete. They both have a reason to want her dead. Besides, Pete didn't seem to notice this, but it sounded like William was awfully positive that Lady Pendleton would die first." Brenda looked hopefully at Mac. "Maybe they presumed she would die first because one or both of them knew she would."

Mac shook his head. He held to the firm belief he had the right person. "Neither of them had a way to get poison of any kind into her food or drink. Besides, we discovered large amounts of antifreeze residue in the cup from Morning Sun."

"What does that have to do with Carrie?" Brenda felt a slow anger rising within her and she fought to control her voice.

"She knew exactly how poisons mixed with other substances. She often visited with Logan on her breaks and she could have easily slipped something into the drink he served. He may or may not have known she put it into the cup." It was as if Mac anticipated her next objection. "I will find out if Carrie was there when the Pendletons came in. Logan probably wouldn't have wanted to mention her being there under the circumstances but I think we have some leverage now."

He was logical, thought Brenda, but she still did not believe Carrie Martin had anything to do with the woman's murder. She said nothing more as Mac parked the car at the police station and they went inside to watch as the new arrivals were processed.

Logan stood waiting to be booked. He glared at Mac.

"Let's go," said the cop. He moved Logan to a room down the hallway.

Brenda watched as the second officer finished processing Carrie. A female officer took her into another room next to the interrogation room where Logan sat.

"I'll go in and see Carrie," said Mac. "The earphones will allow you to listen and you can watch through the one-way window. I think it's best if you don't go in with me since she is an employee of yours. I don't want her to be distracted, or to hold back in any way."

Brenda walked to the window and observed Carrie sitting down. Mac told the officer to remove her handcuffs and stand to the side of the room while Mac began his interrogation. Brenda watched while the initial comments were made and then had an idea.

Brenda asked the deputy to allow her in the room with Logan. When she entered the small room, she noted Logan paced back and forth, agitation clouding his face. He stopped when she came inside.

"I'm not coming to interrogate you. That will be Mac's job. I just want to know why you and Carrie suddenly decided to leave your jobs without telling me or Molly."

"We couldn't stand hearing about Lady Pendleton's death everywhere we turned," he said, practically exploding with frustration. "I was sick of the woman when she lived and happy when she died. She cheated everyone in Sweetfern Harbor and she was hateful toward Carrie. She didn't care who she hurt or what the outcome was, and that includes my own father."

"Tell me what happened to your family."

Anger flared in his eyes as he spoke. "My father was a plumber and a very good one. She hired him to install plumbing work for all the houses she owned and he did a good job. When he was finished she refused to pay him in full for the work he had done. She said he had broken the contract for some small thing that shouldn't have mattered. He had passed up several jobs to get the work done for her. My father barely made ends meet after that. He had spent a lot of money on fixtures and pipes and when she didn't pay him as promised he lost a lot of money on the deal."

"I'm so sorry, Logan. It seems like the more I hear about Lady Pendleton there's just no end to the bitterness and wrath she spread around this town." She paused a moment, glad to see he had calmed a little getting this story out of his system. She then continued carefully. "Have you and Carrie known each other since childhood?"

"I knew her but not well until we had freshman science class together. We clicked right away. Neither of us ever dated anyone else. After her parents died, an aunt of hers from Brooklyn moved in with her, just until Carrie turned eighteen. Soon after she left, that's when Carrie's troubles with Lady Pendleton really started. I knew what would happen to her then."

Logan gave a short, bitter laugh. "Of course, Carrie knew what had happened to my dad, too. Everyone hated that woman." He gestured toward the door emphatically. "She had nothing to do with killing Lady Pendleton. As much as

83

Carrie resented her, she would never have done that. She still wants to be a pharmacist someday. If she had stooped to murder, her chances at that future would be lost. She's better than that."

"What are you trying to tell me, Logan? I have to ask you. Why were you both leaving so suddenly for New York? Was it spur of the moment, or did you plan ahead to do that? I doubt you had a job lined up there."

"I figured I'd find work," he replied defensively. "Kelly promised to help me with that. Carrie was excited to get her education back on track. And, yes, it was spur of the moment," he said. "I mean—we constantly talked about our future but to actually take off like that…Kelly convinced Carrie to come with her." Logan's voice quieted and he seemed lost in thought, staring into the distance as he recalled it to Brenda. "She said it was now or never. Lady Pendleton's death was like a ghost that would never stop haunting us… never stop haunting this town. It was time to get a fresh start. Carrie planned to call you when we got to New York. She said she would come back on weekends and help train someone new. I couldn't let her go alone like that. What if some guy in New York won her over? I had to go with her."

Brenda didn't say anything for a moment. She waited. Something about Logan Tucker told her he was hiding something more. It had something to do with this sudden impulse to run off to New York City.

"It's not like Carrie to just up and leave without any notice. She is more responsible than that."

Logan nodded his head in agreement. "She felt guilty about that but she loves me like I do her. You see…there is nothing left for me here. And Carrie really does love me. She loves me no matter what I've done." He looked up at her with a desperate, pleading look.

Brenda felt shock waves shoot through her. She stood up and raised her hand to stop Logan from saying any more. An officer stood outside the interrogation room and she asked him to stay with Logan. She hurried from the room and signaled to Mac's deputy, who hurried over.

"Tell Detective Rivers I must speak with him right away. He must interrupt his interview; it's that important."

When Mac came out, she told him of her strange conversation with Logan Tucker. "I think he's ready to confess something. He's in distress and he's adamant that Carrie did not do it."

Mac nodded in agreement. "She told me she left like that because Logan wanted to go to New York City, but she wouldn't come out and say why. Now Logan has something to say. She's beginning to make more sense now."

"For the record, I did not interrogate Logan," said Brenda. "I merely had a casual conversation with him about his relationship with Carrie. Once we were talking, he told me how Lady Pendleton ripped off his own family. That was when he made a remark that drew suspicion and I called for you."

"That's all right. It was good that you went in like that. If he had been left alone much longer he would have had too much time to think about his situation and how to get out of it all."

chapter nine

Brenda drew a deep breath. She hoped she was right about Logan Tucker and what he had to say. At the same time, she thought it would be natural for him to point the finger at anyone but himself. He had his whole life ahead of him and a lot to lose. Then again, why had he seemed so ready to reveal his secret to her?

Together, Mac and Brenda went into the room where Logan paced nervously beside the small table. "I understand you are ready to tell me something, Logan. What is it?" Logan twisted his fingers together, stopped as if he was going to speak, but then stopped himself and paced again. "Sit down, Logan. Do you want something to drink? We have soft drinks, water, or coffee if you want anything." Mac appeared relaxed but Brenda noted his alert demeanor. Finally, the young man sat down and shook his head refusing the offer of something to drink.

"Good," said Mac, "now let's get started. Tell me everything you know." He flipped the recorder on. Then he asked Logan if he wanted a lawyer present. When the answer was no, Mac read him his rights again. "Go ahead, then," the detective said.

"I've been working on a motorcycle in my garage. I mean

the garage down the street. My dad has our garage at home piled up with other stuff, so he keeps a couple of things in my garage. Things like jugs of antifreeze." He swallowed hard and continued. "Every day I heard people complaining about how much Lady Pendleton was squeezing them bone dry. I saw it happen to my own dad and we all know what she did to Carrie and to Phyllis. With that lawsuit against Jenny, she was aiming for your daughter too, Mac. You knew something had to be done. Everyone knew something had to be done." He swallowed again. "No one seemed to know what to do about it. I was going crazy thinking it would go on like that forever. So, when I saw no one else was doing anything about her, I did something."

Brenda held her breath. The atmosphere in the little room was close, almost stifling.

"What happened?" asked Mac.

"I knew it was time for her to pick up her coffee beans. That morning before I came to work, I put antifreeze in a little jar and put it in my pocket. She always ordered a cappuccino and so I knew I could be generous with the antifreeze, it would be hidden under the foam. I saw her and William getting out of the car and I started making her drink. I stirred it in well and topped it with a perfect cap of foam. She sat there and drank it and had no idea she was on her way to death. She deserved it."

"How did you know her coffee wouldn't taste wrong to her?"

Logan relaxed. "That was easy. I learned that a long time ago from Carrie in high school chemistry. It has the same chemical composition as sugary drinks or something like that. Who would have known that would come in handy one day?"

"Why would you do such a thing, Logan?" asked Brenda. "You have your whole life ahead of you."

He tilted his chin up, cocky again. "It was simple.

Everyone in Sweetfern Harbor is family to me. I was sick and tired of her beating everyone out of their livelihoods and getting away with it. I was just helping my family. I was just doing what everyone knew needed to be done but no one else had the guts to do." He smiled, though not his usual wide grin. "I'm glad I did it. She didn't deserve to have everything at the expense of the rest of us." He looked at Mac. "I swear to you that Carrie had nothing to do with the murder. She had no idea until I told her a few minutes before we took Kelly to the bus station. That's how I convinced her that the best thing was to leave with Kelly and start a new life in New York without telling anybody." He paused. "Carrie was nowhere near Morning Sun Coffee that day."

He looked at Brenda. "Carrie was at Sheffield House with you that whole morning, remember?" Brenda realized he was right. Carrie had helped her audit her books and there would have been no time in between when she could have been down at the coffee shop.

Mac just shook his head. "Even if you weren't running from the law, running off is a bad idea. Do you know how expensive it is to live in New York? You wouldn't have found support like you do around here. It was a matter of time before we would've found out who killed Lady Pendleton. You wouldn't have lasted in New York City anyway, and running is a red flag for your guilt." He wiped his forehead with the back of his sleeve. "I'm just glad you were honest enough to confess, Logan. Wait right here until my deputy comes in."

While the deputy booked Logan Tucker for the murder of Lady Pendleton, Brenda waited for Carrie. When she came from the interrogation room, Brenda hugged her tightly.

"I'll be calling you back in, Carrie," said Mac, "but for now you are released." He turned and walked to the desk to give instructions to the cop sitting behind the desk.

"Come on, Carrie, let's get some fresh air," said Brenda.

"We'll walk home. Mac has other things he needs to take care of right now."

Neither woman mentioned Logan's name but Brenda could see the deep sadness in Carrie's eyes. They didn't speak and together left the police station and turned to walk to the bed and breakfast. Mac would have to find out how much Carrie Martin knew, and when, but that would come later. Right now, Brenda needed to take care of her.

By the time they returned to Sheffield Bed and Breakfast, everyone was in the dining room for dinner.

Carrie looked blankly toward the happy din of conversation coming from the dining room, then turned to Brenda. "I have no appetite." Brenda patted her arm and gave her another hug.

"Get a good night's sleep, Carrie. If you want anything later come down and help yourself."

Everyone at the table greeted Brenda and she apologized for being late. No one asked about Carrie. Word was beginning to spread through Sweetfern Harbor that there had been an arrest in the murder of Lady Pendleton. Brenda felt sure that even though no one knew who had been arrested, the news would make the rounds before bedtime. Logan had chosen Edward Graham to defend him. She did her best to eat and make normal conversation despite the eventful interrogation that had lasted all afternoon.

When Brenda returned to her apartment after dinner her cell phone rang. Mac Rivers told her that one more mystery was solved. It turned out to have been Kelly Martin who mentioned the locked desk drawer to Logan.

"Logan told me that Kelly found it a curious thing and she and Carrie jokingly wondered what you locked in there. Logan took it as a challenge. They laughed when he told them he could find out. They never dreamed he would actually break in and search through the drawer. He took the contents with him because he was worried they incriminated him. I think he was disappointed when nothing of interest was there. He is not only being held for the murder of Lady Pendleton but also for breaking and entering." Mac paused for a few seconds. "He thought maybe he could use your notes to prepare in case he had to answer too many questions. As it turned out, he found nothing specific against him. He tore up the notes and threw them in a dumpster."

They hung up and Brenda turned her TV on. Every local channel had breaking news. Logan Tucker had confessed to the murder of Priscilla Pendleton. Details were not given except that he confessed to Detective Mac Rivers of Sweetfern Harbor how the murder occurred. According to the news, the detective stated they had much more work to do on the case. Brenda knew they would have to have evidence that correlated with Logan's confession in case he took it all back. They had to find the jar Logan used and determine for certain the source of the antifreeze. She had no doubt Mac's team was searching Logan's apartment that very moment.

Brenda turned the TV off and opened her window. The sounds of the ocean waves soothed her and she lay down to rest her tired body. She drew in a long breath and savored the sea smells. The bed and breakfast was quiet. Seagulls settled down and only a few songbirds called from the trees. She fell into a deep and dreamless sleep.

When Brenda came downstairs the next morning, voices buzzed over breakfast even more than usual. Carrie was in her office. She appeared to be working on reservations that had come in overnight, but her eyes were sunken as if she had not slept, and she wouldn't meet Brenda's eyes.

"Did you eat breakfast, Carrie?" Brenda asked her.

"I'm not hungry," Carrie replied absently, tapping slowly at the keyboard.

"You didn't eat dinner last night. Carrie, look at me," Brenda pleaded. The young woman looked up at her guiltily. "If you want to help Logan, you will need to keep your strength up. Join me for breakfast and we can chat about business. I'll keep you from the gossips, don't worry."

Carrie smiled weakly. "You're right. And I appreciate a diversion."

When they walked down the short hallway to the dining room entry, voices hushed momentarily. Carrie smiled at the guests and said to Phyllis, who stood near the door, "It's all right. I don't want you to feel you have to step on eggshells around me."

Phyllis patted her arm. "You can count on all of us in Sweetfern Harbor to do everything to support Logan. Tell us what you need from us."

"I will let you know. I hope to get to visit him sometime today but for now, Brenda and I are going to have our breakfast."

Brenda was sure Carrie would not be allowed to see Logan any time soon. Her life was about to get much more complicated, according to Mac Rivers. But for now, Brenda kept her promise to Carrie and kept the conversation light and simple as they dove into plates heaped with scrambled eggs, fresh bagels, and strips of bacon. Brenda reached for the coffeepot on the sideboard and poured them steaming cups of coffee as they talked about the bed and breakfast.

"Phyllis mentioned two of the rooms need some updating," said Carrie. "Phyllis has some wonderful ideas about decorating, you know she's the one who helped your uncle with things like that for many years."

Brenda agreed to speak with her housekeeper. After an hour lingering at the table, they went back to the front desk. Brenda saw Phyllis dusting in the sitting room and joined her. They chatted about the updates needed in two of the rooms on the second floor.

"We're booked until the end of summer," said Brenda, "but I will let Carrie know not to book any more guests into those two rooms until we can get them redone. It will be September by the time that happens."

Brenda decided to spend her day taking care of her bed and breakfast. Detective work could wait for further developments. She would let Mac tell Carrie she was not allowed to visit her boyfriend behind bars.

chapter ten

A full twenty-four hours passed before Brenda spoke with Mac again. It sounded as if he needed a break, too.

"Let's take an evening out, Brenda, if you have time," he said.

Once again, her heart skipped a beat. What was it about this man who could one minute frustrate her and in the next moment, draw her to him like a magnet? She was more than ready to have a night out with him.

"It looks like you and Mac may have something going," said Phyllis. She winked at Carrie who stood nearby.

"We are simply taking a little time away from this case. I'm sure Mac needs the break." She glanced at Carrie. "I think Logan has found a good lawyer when it comes to Edward."

Carrie smiled. "I hope he is good for Logan. It makes me feel better about this whole thing. I'm going to try and see Logan in a little while."

An hour later, Carrie returned. From the look on her face, Brenda knew Mac or someone in the department had given her the bad news. She returned to her office without a word.

The guests in the two rooms needing repairs had checked out. Brenda took advantage of the time before the next guests checked in later that day. She and Phyllis looked at the room together. There were no cracks in the walls but they needed a good coat of paint, perhaps in a new color. The bathroom tile needed replacing and Brenda decided new bedspreads and curtains were needed as well. She made notes as Phyllis suggested a few ideas she had been thinking of to help give the rooms that special Sheffield touch.

"In September, we'll get started on the work. It shouldn't take more than two days for both rooms unless we see something unexpected." The rest of the day, Brenda tried to busy herself with tasks and not fret too much about Carrie, whose eyes were rimmed with red from crying and whom she didn't know how to comfort.

Later that evening, she tried to clear her mind and focus on her date with Mac Rivers. Though she admitted to herself it was technically their second dinner date, she had no intentions of satisfying Phyllis Lindsey's suspicions that it was.

When Mac picked her up around seven, he looked more handsome than ever. He wore khakis and a Polo shirt. The casual look enhanced his looks more than ever. She had carefully applied her usual light makeup and felt good about the way her summer dress showed off her figure. At forty-six years old she knew she still looked appealing.

They sat down at a table outside an upscale bistro located several miles from Sweetfern Harbor in the next town. The restaurant overlooked the ocean and beach. Everyone around them was laid back and conversations flowed easily.

"This is beautiful," said Brenda. "How long have you known of this spot?"

"I'm glad you like it and hope you don't mind when I tell you this is where I met my wife over twenty years ago. She was with someone else and didn't look happy with him. I made sure I accidently bumped her chair when I passed their table. Our eyes locked and I managed to get her telephone number before the night was over," he said with a twinkle in his eye.

Brenda laughed. "How did you manage that without her date knowing it?"

"I waited until he went to the bar for more drinks and asked her for it. The rest is history, as they say."

"From the sounds of it, I take it that it all worked out for both of you."

"Yes, it did," he said, suddenly wistful. "We had a happy life together. But it was cut too short when her illness hit her. Jenny and I had a lot of support from everyone in Sweetfern Harbor. If we hadn't had that, I don't know what we would have done. I had a lot to learn about day-to-day parenting of a daughter."

In the comfortable silence, Brenda turned to gaze at the ocean. The rays of the setting sun behind them reflected on the water. She wondered how it happened that she had never found anyone she wanted to make a life with. Mac and his wife had been lucky. Her thoughts were interrupted by his voice.

"I don't want to talk too much about Logan's case, Brenda, but in Sweetfern Harbor, everyone is family. Without exception, they will rally around him. Some are searching for loopholes as I speak. I know that because that is what they do for one another."

"What do you mean?"

"I'm saying not everything is about the letter of the law when it comes to Sweetfern Harbor. I just don't want you to be disappointed if we've put in all this hard work and it takes a new twist."

Brenda smiled. "I have noticed how close-knit the town is so I'm not surprised at what you say. I promise I won't be disappointed."

She hoped he would take that as understanding and move

on to another subject. He scrutinized her face, seeming to take her at her word.

They discussed the menu and while waiting for their dinner, they watched and commented on the people walking along the beach. Mac regaled her with a hilarious story about rescuing a baby duck from the harbor one chilly autumn night. It was a beautiful night, and she felt lucky to be sitting in the company of a handsome man. She liked his laugh, and his stories, and she liked how he looked at her when he thought she wasn't looking.

After their meal, they walked down the steps to the beach and joined others strolling along the sand. The night was perfect and Brenda felt Mac's warmth when their arms or shoulders touched while they walked along.

As the week went by, Brenda was aware of things happening in the town. A lawyer from out of town was hired to help Edward Graham prepare Logan's defense. A short time later, Pete Graham stopped in at Morning Sun Coffee as Brenda sat at the window with Phyllis. Pete joined them.

"Have you heard the judge on Logan's case was moved to another jurisdiction?"

"Oh no," said Phyllis, "I hope that doesn't mean the next one assigned to his case will be harsh with him."

Pete swayed on his heels. "Nope," he said, "apparently it means the case will probably be thrown out. I heard that from dad. The lawyer he brought in on the case to help him has clout with the jurisdiction board that decides these things. He somehow maneuvered things around and suddenly this new judge is in town."

"What grounds will he have to dismiss the case?" Brenda asked.

Pete shrugged his shoulders. "I guess since the whole

town is willing to testify on Logan's behalf, plus the fact that William has uncovered a few illegal dealings his wife had, all adds up in Logan's favor."

"I can't wait to tell Carrie the good news," said Phyllis.

"She already knows it. Mac even let her talk with Logan a little while ago. I guess he finally realized Carrie didn't play any part in the whole deal." Pete Graham looked smug.

Brenda realized Mac Rivers meant it when he said that not everything followed the letter of the law when it comes to Sweetfern Harbor. She supposed in the end, if what Pete told them was true, then Logan Tucker would probably have a future after all.

While everyone offered opinions around the table, Brenda noticed Mac pulling up in his car. He parked in the one spot still open in front of the coffee shop and came in. He went directly to the group and turned to Brenda.

"Can we use Sheffield Bed and Breakfast for a meeting right away?" Mac had such a serious look on his face that Brenda didn't ask questions, she just nodded. "Everyone else gather people together. Edward Graham has an announcement."

When all were assembled on the side lawn of her property, Brenda was not surprised to see that the entire town had shown up. Fleeting thoughts of stranded tourists crossed her mind knowing shops were closed.

Edward stepped forward. "I want to tell all of you that I have drawn up new lease documents for you. But that's not the big news here. William, with the court's approval, wants it known that rents have been rolled back to where they were ten years ago, and will not be raised for another ten years." A joyful murmur raced through the crowd. "I would like to personally take this opportunity to thank Detective Mac Rivers, his department, and Miss Brenda Sheffield for their tireless work in solving the case of Lady Pendleton's untimely death. An added note is that I feel sure my client Logan will be given a lighter sentence, or possibly probation, for his part in what happened," he finished with a knowing chuckle.

In reality, Brenda knew that the lawyer knew Logan Tucker's slate would be wiped completely clean.

Edward Graham waved his hand to silence the crowd's noisy approval of this announcement. "I have something else of importance. As you know, Carrie Martin has decided to move to New York City and finish her studies. Well, when Brenda heard about this plan, once again everyone chipped in to help pay her way until she can get on her feet." As Carrie stood with a dumbfounded look on her face, Edward Graham handed her an envelope and bent over to whisper the amount in her ear. The assembled crowd clapped and cheered as Carrie threw her arms around the distinguished older lawyer's neck in gratitude.

A taxi pulled into the driveway at that moment. Everyone rushed to Carrie and hugged her before she tore herself away and got into the cab with her suitcase. The crowd mingled and several wiped their eyes. People shuffled up to Edward and the new lease documents were handed out one by one.

Brenda went inside the bed and breakfast to think about the lawyer's words. Jenny Rivers followed her in. She handed Brenda a huge bouquet of mixed blooms.

"My father picked this out for you a little while ago. He asked me to deliver it to you. Do you want to hear the message that goes along with the bouquet?"

"Yes, I do," said Brenda, inhaling the sweet fragrance of the flowers.

"He said the only message with the flowers is 'Welcome to the Sweetfern Harbor family.'" Jenny grinned. "See, I told you that you two would make a good pair."

Brenda laughed. "Don't get your hopes up...but I do enjoy his company."

Jenny grinned with sudden glee. "Why don't you tell him that yourself?"

Brenda turned to see the detective standing in the doorway, watching Brenda's reaction. "I heard your words, Brenda, and I thank you. Now let's go for a long drive along the highway and watch the seagulls dip in and out of the water."

He reached for her hand. Brenda took his hand with satisfaction and smiled.

.

more from wendy

Alaska Cozy Mystery Series

Maple Hills Cozy Series

Sweeetfern Harbor Cozy Series

Sweet Peach Cozy Series

Sweet Shop Cozy Series

Twin Berry Bakery Series

about wendy meadows

Wendy Meadows is a USA Today bestselling author whose stories showcase women sleuths. To date, she has published dozens of books, which include her popular Sweetfern Harbor series, Sweet Peach Bakery series, and Alaska Cozy series, to name a few. She lives in the "Granite State" with her husband, two sons, two mini pigs and a lovable Labradoodle.

Join Wendy's newsletter to stay up-to-date with new releases. As a subscriber, you'll also get BLACKVINE MANOR, the complete series, for FREE!

Join Wendy's Newsletter Here
wendymeadows.com/cozy

Made in United States
North Haven, CT
29 July 2023